Also by Greer Rylie

- Petals & Steel
- Before Autumn Ends
- Her Accidental Fiancé
- Something More
- Mended Hearts

Welcome to
Leather Persuasion Resort.
Where all your wildest fantasies
can become a
reality.

Chapter 1

"This can't be happening. No fucking way is this happening right now." Pulling to the side of the road, Skyler looked down at herself before groaning and lowering her head to the steering wheel. "This is just perfect." Drawing in a deep breath, she sat up and looked at the screen on her dash. The temperature readout caused her stomach to clench, and she looked down at herself again before grasping the door handle and pushing the door open. Heat instantly flooded the interior of the car and she seriously considered just shutting the door and driving the rest of the way on a flat. Shaking her head, she pulled up on the button to release the trunk and stepped out of the car into the heat. Raising her hand to shield her eyes from the sun, she looked in both directions before closing the door and walking to the back of the car. Lifting the trunk lid, she pulled out the spare tire and leaned in to retrieve the jack and lug wrench. The deep rumble of an engine reached her ears and her breath caught in her throat. *Please drive on by.* The words repeated in her mind, and she closed her eyes as she gritted her teeth when the engine grew silent behind her. "This is going from bad to worse."

"Aren't you hot?"

Easing to an upright position, Skyler looked over her shoulder and glared at the muscular chest standing a few feet away. Tilting her head back, she stared at the mirrored sunglasses covering his eyes. "Excuse me?"

Dipping his head, the man lowered his sunglasses with one finger and peered at her over the top of them. "You realize it's damn near a hundred and ten degrees out here, right?"

"What's your point?"

His eyes traveled the length of her body before he met her gaze again. "You're wearing a trench coat."

Crossing her arms beneath her breasts, Skyler turned to face him fully and lifted her chin defiantly. "Again, what's your point?"

Lifting his hands in a surrendering gesture, he took a step back and smiled down at her. "No point. Just stating the obvious, I guess." Mimicking her stance, he finally looked at her spare tire and nodded towards it. "You need any help with your flat?"

It was on the tip of her tongue to tell him no, but the sweat trickling down her naked back had her swallowing down her bitter reply. Chewing the inside of her cheek, she gave him a brief nod and quickly stepped to the side when he began walking towards her. "Thank you."

"Not a problem." Reaching into the trunk, he grasped the jack and lug wrench and pulled them out. "This is going to take a few minutes. You sure you don't want to take off that trench coat?"

Skyler realized she was fanning herself and dropped her hand to her side. "No. I'm fine."

"You sure about that? Your face is turning a very unhealthy shade of red." Squatting in front of the flat tire, he began to loosen the lug nuts as he looked up at her and waited for her response.

Clutching the lapels of the trench coat, she wrapped her other arm over her stomach and took another step back, wincing and crying out when the heel of her boot came down on a rock and twisted beneath her. Pain shot up her leg and her arms pinwheeled as she tried to keep her balance. Her eyes widened when strong warm fingers wrapped around her left wrist and jerked her forward, slamming her nose into the man's muscular chest. Her breathing quickened as she drew in his intoxicating scent.

"Are you okay?"

Her face heated with embarrassment, and she nodded against his chest, drawing in his scent again before pushing out of his embrace. "I'm fine, thank you."

He stared down at her bowed head for a few seconds before dropping his hands and stepping back. "Maybe you should wait in the car."

Her head snapped up and she almost threw herself into his arms again as relief washed through her body. "Are you sure? Is that even safe?"

A smile lifted the corner of his mouth and he looked at her coat again. "I'm sure. Just sit still when I get the car up on the jack."

Skyler hesitated before shaking her head. She wanted nothing more in that moment than to crawl back inside her car and blast the air conditioner, but the risk was too great. "I'll just sit over there under the trees until you finish, if that's okay." When he nodded, she gave him a weak smile and limped across the road to the stand of trees.

"Okay, you're ready to go."

Cracking open her eyes, Skyler squinted as she stared up at the man. "What do I owe you?" Waving away his outstretched hand, she used the tree behind her to help her stand and avoided eye contact as she applied her weight to her ankle.

"Nothing. I'm happy I could help."

Lifting her head, Skyler pressed her lips together and held out her hand. "Well, thank you for helping me, Mr..." When he placed his hand in hers, she gave his fingers a slight squeeze, and began to regret her decision to shake hands when he held on as she tried to pull away.

"Quinn. My name is Quinn. And you would be...?"

Tugging her hand back, she finally broke his hold on her. "Why?"

He stared down at her in silence for a bit before sighing and turning to walk away, lifting a hand and waving over his shoulder. "Glad I could help you, ma'am."

Skyler watched him straddle his motorcycle, berating herself for treating him so harshly when all he did was change her tire. Stepping from beneath the trees, she opened her mouth to tell him her name, but the words died on her tongue as the powerful engine roared to life. She watched him pull out into the street and lifted her hand slowly when he waved again as he sped away. Hurrying across the road, she quickly got back inside her car and started the engine. Sky winced and rolled down her window as hot air from the car vents blasted her in the face. Wiping sweat from her brow, she fanned herself with her hand as she waited for the air to turn cold. Reaching for the gearshift, her hand stopped in mid-air as she caught a glimpse of white sticking out from beneath her windshield wiper. Opening the car door again, she stepped out enough to pick up the card. Sitting back down in the driver's seat, she closed the car door and turned the card over, her lips moving as she silently read the words on the front.

Kennedy Auto Repair, Quinn Kennedy - Owner

The number listed below the address was scratched out and replaced with a handwritten number and the words, *Come by and get your tire fixed,* scrawled beneath the number. Tapping the card on the steering wheel, Skyler slowly smiled before putting it in her coat pocket and dropping the car into gear.

Chapter 2

Staring down at the plane ticket in her hand, Skyler's mouth opened and closed as she tried to formulate words.

"It's great, right?" When she raised her eyes to stare at him, he winked and lifted his glass of whiskey to his lips. "I can tell you're excited by how speechless you are."

Holding the ticket out, she shook it until he took it from her. "Ben, we've talked about this. I told you I wasn't going to Peru with you." Walking across the room, she stopped by the front door and stepped into her heels before lifting her bag from the entry table. "You always do this. I tell you no about something and you do it anyway."

"Yeah, and you usually end up going along with

it. So what's the big damn deal about Peru?" Slamming the last of the whiskey back, he rolled the glass with his fingers and stared at her through angry eyes. "You fucking around with someone else, is that it?"

Rolling her eyes at him, she shook her head as she opened the door and walked out into the hallway without answering. Stopping in front of the elevator, she pressed the lobby button and turned to stare at the door she had just walked out of. She knew he'd follow her, she expected him to demand that she return to the suite and finish what they had started. But, when he casually stepped out into the hallway with his phone to his ear and a smirk playing over his lips, she knew it was over. "You wouldn't dare."

Arching an eyebrow, he smiled and lowered his voice into a sultry tone she knew all too well. "Nancy, how have you been? I know it's been awhile, but I was wondering if you'd like to a take trip with me?" His smile grew wider, and he turned to walk back into his suite.

Skyler heard the deadbolt fall into place and she lifted her middle finger at the closed door before stepping into the elevator.

"So, it's really over between you and Ben?"

Skyler nodded and pressed down on the remote control's channel button. "Yep. And good riddance. I'm just sorry I never found out what kind of a person he was sooner"

"What are you going to do now?"

Looking at her sister from the corner of her eye, she pointed the remote towards her bedroom door. "Throw that fucking trench coat away, for starters."

Sunni giggled and covered her mouth when Skyler glared at her. "Come on, Sky. You know the story is still funny."

"It wasn't funny three months ago and it's not funny now." When Sunni laughed again, Skyler threw down the remote and stood up, her arms crossed beneath her breasts as she glared down at her sister. "You remember the part where I was butt ass naked beneath that coat, right?"

Sunni wiggled her eyebrows playfully. "Yeah I do. I also remember you said this Quinn guy was sexy as hell." Gasping, she jumped up and grabbed Skyler by the upper arms. "You should call him!"

Shrugging free of Sunni's hold, she shook her head and spun on her heel. "No way in hell. The man thought I was weird for standing in the blazing sun in a trench coat. He's not going to want to hear from me, I can promise you that."

Following Skyler into the kitchen, Sunni leaned against the door frame and crossed one foot over the other. "You don't know that. Besides, what would it hurt? You said he wrote a note on the card that said, *Come by and get your tire fixed.* The man practically begged you to call him."

"The answer is no, Sunshine. As daddy used to say when we asked to go out on a school night, *it ain't happening, kid.* Besides, it wasn't that kind of a note. He own's the place and it's his job." Washing her hands, she pulled open the refrigerator door and peered inside. She was reaching for a pizza box when the doorbell rang followed by a rapid knock. Pulling the box out, she handed it to her sister on her way to the front door. "Heat that up, will ya?"

"Ummm, sure?"

Reaching the front door, she pulled it open and stared out in confusion. Leaning out, she looked left and right before looking down at the package sitting on the porch. Cautiously picking it up, she read the sender's name and smothered a laugh with the back of her hand.

"Who's it from?"

Clutching the package to her chest, she turned to face Sunni with a toothy grin. "Just something I ordered and forgot about." She scowled and turned to the side when Sunni reached for the package. "Get back."

"Come on, Sky. Let me see it." Sunni poked her bottom lip out and batted her lashes at her sister.

"Uh huh. You're so nosey." Side-stepping her sister again, Skyler took the package into her room and dropped it into the top drawer of her dresser before walking back out into the hallway and pulling the door closed. Seeing the look in Sunni's eyes, she turned the skeleton key in the lock before removing it and slipping the chain it was attached to over her head.

Crossing her arms beneath her breasts, Sunni tapped her tiny foot and screwed her mouth up in a scowling pout. "You saying you don't trust me?"

Laughing, Skyler nodded and patted her sister's cheek playfully. "That's exactly what I'm saying." When Sunni continued to glare up at her, she nudged her with her hip to get her walking. "Let's go eat that pizza before it gets cold again."

"Who's Lacy?"

Confusion pulled Skyler's brow down and she cast a quick glance over her shoulder. "Who?"

Sunni raised hr eyebrows and pointed back toward Skyler's bedroom door. "The name on the package. It looked like is said Lacy something. So who's Lacy?"

"It's a... boutique one of my friend's told me about."

"You hesitated. Why'd you hesitate? Is it naughty or something?" Sunni hurried after Skyler, a teasing smile playing across her lips. "What is it? Is it a dildo?"

Swallowing down another fit of laughter, Skyler walked into the kitchen and washed her hands again before sitting down at the table and giving her sister a small smile. "Maybe I'll tell you about it later."

Walking from the bathroom, Skyler was singing along to the song emitting from the overhead speakers and drying her hair when her eyes landed on her dresser. Lowering the towel, she looked towards her closed bedroom door, wondering if Sunni was asleep yet. Clucking her tongue, she softly chided herself as she walked over to stand in front of the dresser. "It's your house and the door is locked." Still, she slowly pulled the dresser drawer open and darted a quick glance towards her bedroom door again when the drawer made a loud squeaking noise. Holding her breath, she waited for Sunni to knock on the door and ask what she was doing. After a few minutes of silence, she reached inside and lifted the package out. Tiptoeing across the room to her bed, she sat the package down on top of her pillow and stared at it, her fingers twisting together nervously in front of her. She knew what lay inside the package. She had ordered it specifically for a night with Ben, but now... now she wondered if she would ever get to wear it.

Drawing a deep breath through her nose, she sat down on the bed and pulled the package towards her. Flipping it over, she unwrapped the box and removed the tape that sealed it together before easing the flaps of the box open and pushing the tissue paper to the side. Her breath caught as she stared down at the custom made leather corset nestled inside. Reaching into the box, she lifted the corset out, ignoring the white envelope that had been lying beneath it, and rubbed the butter-soft leather with the pads of her thumbs. Lifting it to her face, she closed her eyes and smiled as she pressed the leather against her cheek. A squeal of excitement lodged in her throat, and she jumped to her feet as she untied her bathrobe, her gaze never leaving the corset as she let the robe fall to the floor.

Wrapping the corset around her waist, she held her breath as she fastened the busk together before reaching back and pulling on the laces until the leather hugged her curves. Tying it off, she ran her hands over her stomach before walking over to the full-length mirror sitting in the corner of the room. Looking at her reflection, she let her gaze travel the length of her body and squeezed her legs together as she stared at the juncture of her thighs.

The corset set perfectly on her hips, the back ties just barely grazing over her bare flesh. Turning away from the mirror, she walked over to the bed and sat down beside the box. She lightly ran her fingertips over the tops of her thighs and stifled a moan when her thumbs grazed the cleft of her womanhood. She was pushing the box away when she noticed the envelope. Picking it up, she opened it and pulled out the note inside.

> *Thank you for your order.*
> *Daisy told me you might be interested*
> *in going to a resort we are a part of, so*
> *I've enclosed a detailed description of it. If*
> *you are interested, shoot me an email and*
> *I'll give you the name and location.*
> *Once again, Thanks for your order and*
> *I wish you many satisfying adventures.*
> *Lacy's Apparel and More*

Tugging on the lace of the corset, Skyler loosened the laces and unfastened the busk, sighing as she took it off and laid it back in the box. Standing, she returned the box to her dresser drawer and lifted out a pair of lacy underwear and slid the drawer closed. Pulling the panties on, she picked up her night shirt and walked back to the bed, shrugging it on and pulling the covers back before crawling in. Picking up the envelope she removed the other sheet of paper from inside and hesitated briefly before flipping it open. As she read the description of the resort, her eyes grew wide, and a smile tugged at the corners of her mouth.

Chapter 3

Skyler took a sip from the glass of wine she had been handed when she stepped onto the cabin cruiser and leaned against the railing as she watched the boat dock fade into the distance. Her heart raced with anticipation of what she was doing and where she was going. She had never been to a resort much less one like Lacy had described in her note. She wondered if they had received her reply to the questionnaire she had been sent when she contacted them and berated herself for not following up with them before leaving. Her heart raced again, this time with a twinge of fear, when she remembered some of the questions that had been on the questionnaire. Taking another sip, she swallowed before releasing a nervous sigh. *I really hope they've received my responses.*

Shouts from behind her drew her attention and she turned in time to see one of the crew members pointing off to the right. Looking in that direction, she noticed a speedboat rapidly approaching. A slight touch on her elbow drew her attention away from the approaching speed boat and she turned to face the handsome crew member standing behind her. "Excuse me, Miss. I'm going to need you to go to your cabin now."

Worry blossomed in her chest, and she looked back at the speed boat briefly before following the crew member. "Is everything all right? Are we about to be attacked or something?"

"No, nothing as dramatic and exciting as that, I assure you. We've just been informed that one of our other guests has arrived late and we are stopping to allow them to board. I assume you'd be more comfortable being out of sight, no?" His smile was friendly and his tone soft as he waved a hand towards the small room she had been assigned.

Returning his smile, she held out the wine glass to him and entered the room before replying. "You would be correct. Thank you." When he gave a slight bow and turned to leave, she gently touched his arm. "Excuse me, but can you tell me how long it will be before we arrive? I'd like to take a nap if there's time."

Smiling, he patted her hand before stepping back. "It will take some time to get there. You have time for a brief nap. When shall I wake you?"

Glancing at the watch on her wrist, she noted the time and looked back up at him. "About four pm?"

Dipping his head in a slight nod, he turned and walked away, leaving Skyler standing in the doorway staring after him. When he disappeared around a corner, she closed the cabin room door and turned to survey the small room before walking over to her bunk and laying down. As she lay there, listening to the crew moving over head, she thought about all the things she planned to experience while at the resort. Her eyes grew heavy, and she was drifting off to sleep when a vaguely familiar male voice spoke just outside her room. Mumbling softly, she rolled over, pulled the pillow over her head, and drifted off into a deeper sleep.

A rapid knocking jerked Skyler from sleep and she sat up quickly. Her heart raced as she pushed her hair back and stared around in confusion. Panic began to set in before her mind cleared and she remembered where she was and where she was going. Her eyes widened when the knocking came again followed by a deep voice.

"Miss? Are you okay?"

Jumping from the bed, she stepped to the door and pressed her ear to the wood. "Yes. What's happened?"

There was silence from the other side for a second before the man spoke again. "We've docked a few miles from the resort. Are you ready to go ashore now?"

Skyler turned to look at the small window above her bunk and her brow pulled down in confusion. Looking at her wristwatch, her mouth dropped open in shock as she noted the time. Jerking the door open, she stared up at the crew member standing there. "I asked to be awakened at four, it's after ten pm."

The man nodded once and laced his fingers together. "Yes, Miss. We tried to wake you several times, but you never responded to our calls."

Skyler's eyebrows shot up and she turned to pick up her cellphone, her finger swiping over the screen. "I don't have any missed calls."

Lifting a hand, the man remained silent as he pointed inside the room.

Turning, Skyler saw the small white phone peeking out from beneath her bag, the cord laying curled up on the floor. Releasing a heavy sigh, she turned and leaned her head against the edge of the door as she looked back at the crew member, her cheeks flushed with embarrassment. "Looks like I accidentally disconnected it." When he gave her a soft smile, she straightened and cleared her throat before speaking. "Give me five minutes?"

"Yes, Miss. You can come to the top when you are ready, and Scottie will escort you ashore." Turning, he sauntered away, stopping a few doors down and knocking before turning the knob and walking inside. "Sir, we've..."

Closing her own door, Skyler reached for her bag

and rummaged through it as she stepped into the tiny bathroom.

Stepping up onto the dock, Skyler was thankful for the dim lights on either side of the dock. Heat rushed to her face the instant she saw the impeccably dressed man standing a few feet away and she knew her face was tinged pink. Touching one of her cheeks, she looked at her feet and licked her suddenly dry lips before smiling and looking back up at him. He was the most beautiful man she had seen to date. She noticed one perfectly sculpted brow lift and it was only then that she realized he was holding out his hand towards her. Her eyes widened and she hastily held her bag out for him. "Sorry."

Chuckling, he gave his head a slight shake before glancing over her shoulder and tilting his head at the bag she was holding out.

Skyler closed her eyes and groaned, mortified that she had just tried to give her bag to the first man she met. Opening her eyes again, she pointed over her shoulder at the boat she arrived in not two minutes ago. "I should probably save us all from any further embarrassment and just go on back home now."

"It's quite all right." When she gently cupped his hand, he lifted her fingers to his mouth and brushed her knuckles with a featherlight kiss before releasing her and turning to follow the young man carrying her bags. "I hope your journey here was a pleasant one. I'm the Director of Guest Relations, Master Lance. I have taken the liberty of arranging transportation to your cottage."

"To be honest, I slept most of the way. But before that it was okay. I mean, we made it, so..." Realizing she was babbling, she clamped her mouth shut and looked up in time to keep from running into his back. Stopping, she opened her mouth to apologize a third time as he turned to look down at her.

"Miss..."

"Skyl... umm, just Sky."

Dipping his head in acknowledgment, he studied her briefly before continuing. "There's really no need to be nervous, Sky. This is a safe place. No harm will come to you without your permission."

Sky returned his playful smile before swallowing past the lump in her throat and looking at her surroundings. Twisting her fingers nervously in front of her, she met his gaze again and spoke in a soft whisper. "I... I've never done this before."

"Which is why I will make sure you are paired with someone who will be sensitive to your wants and needs. We aim to make every experience pleasurable and unforgettable." Taking her by the elbow he walked the few remaining feet to the awaiting jeep and helped her inside. "You'll find a welcome packet in your cottage. Should you need anything or have any questions before I see you again, feel free to call me."

Skyler's gaze remained glued to his face as he closed the door and stepped away from the jeep. She had so many questions about the resort and a tiny seed of doubt made her stomach churn as the chauffeur shifted the jeep into gear and pressed down on the gas pedal.

Chapter 4

"Master Q. It's a pleasure to see you again."

Quinn took the papers that Lance held out to him and memorized the name at the top of the page. "Is she as dainty as her name indicates?"

Lance's teeth were a brilliant white when he smiled across the desk at Quinn. "She's absolutely adorable, but not at all as her name implies." With one well-manicured finger, he slid another paper across the desk. "This is her first journey into the BDSM lifestyle, but I think she'll be quite an enjoyable match for you."

Picking up the paper, Quinn read down the list and deep laughter filled the room when he got to the bottom. "Oh, this should be fun."

"I know you'll take very good care of her and do

everything you can to make her experience an enjoyable one. But..."

Quinn looked up from the paper and arched an eyebrow. "But? Is there more I should know?"

Sitting forward, Lance laced his long fingers together in front of him on the desk and held Quinn's gaze. "I feel she's, well, different from what she's written there."

Quinn looked back at the paper, his mouth turning down at the corners. "What makes you say that?"

"Mistress Thea said she's understandably nervous but very curious and open to trying many things. Though, I suspect she won't be too receptive of some of those. But, as I stated, I know you'll take very good care of her." Leaning back in his chair, he studied his nails as he waited for Quinn to respond.

Getting to his feet, Quinn folded the papers and turned toward the door. "I'll pay a visit to her in the morning and go from there." Stopping with his hand on the door knob, Quinn looked back at the man sitting behind the desk. "Who is to be her mentor?" When he received no answer, he lowered his gaze to the floor before nodding and walking from the office.

Quinn sat on the deck of his cottage and sipped from his whiskey tumbler as he studied the list in his hand. He chuckled again as he read the handwritten notes along the edge. The woman had started out marking Y for yes and N for No but half-way through she switched to completely marking through most of the list. Reaching the bottom of the page, he smiled as he read the note she had written.

First, my safe word is Vanilla. I just want to get that established right away.

Now, while this list covers a lot of things, most of which I've scratched out, I do have my own set of rules. If my rules are an issue, please let me know and I will go home.

I want pleasure and pain. I want to be punished but not hurt. I won't take abuse from anyone. I want to be desired but out of reach. I don't like being ordered around, and I'm not going to be treated as if I'm just a toy to be discarded at the end of the day. No sex! I'm not saying never, but I am saying not now. Sex play, yes. Penetration, not right away.

Quinn looked out at the beach and sipped from his whisky glass. He was used to receiving demands, but none that were so straight forward. Looking down at the list again, he dropped his feet from the railing to the deck and stood, before walking inside his cottage and going to his closet. Pulling the doors open, he stared the clothes hanging inside and selected a pair of blue jeans and a black tee shirt before lifting a braided leather belt off the hook on the door. Walking towards the bathroom, he laid the list on the desk and checked the time before stepping into the bathroom and closing the door.

Chapter 5

Skyler was chewing on a piece of bacon and reading over the papers Thea had left with her when her phone vibrated near her elbow. Picking it up, she turned it over and read the text sent from her friend, Daisy.

DAISY:

So, how do you like it?

Wiping her fingers on her napkin, she considered her words before tapping out a reply.

Skyler:

I haven't been out of my room yet, Daisy.

DAISY:

Girl, what are you waiting for?
There's so much to do on the
island.

SKYLER:

Are you aware of the type of place
Leather Persuasion is, ma'am?

DAISY:

Of course I do. It's a nice resort.
Why do you think I had Lacy send
you the information about it?

SKYLER:

Oh for fucks sake, Daisy. Have you
ever been here?

Skyler bounced her leg in anger as she waited for her friend to reply. When the phone rang and displayed Daisy's number, she scowled at it and debated letting it go straight to voicemail. Breathing deeply through her nose, she swiped a finger across the screen and placed the phone to her ear. "I'm taking this call as a no."

"*Actually, yes, I have been there. Multiple times. I just didn't want to say so in a text. Have you met Vincent yet? Oh what am I saying? Of course you have. Isn't he dreamy?*"

"He's off limits."

"Then you haven't had an in-depth conversation with him yet. He can do things to you that you never knew you wanted. He's a master with his ton..."

Skyler cut her off before she could finish her sentence. "That's not what I mean. I'm saying, he's not for me."

"But..."

"No buts. I'll know him when I meet him. *If* I meet him."

"You'll miss out on a lot of living if you keep waiting for 'the one' Sky."

Skyler smiled into the phone as she looked towards the leather corset lying across the foot of her bed. "I didn't say I wasn't willing to test the waters, now did I?" Daisy's laughter caused Skyler to wince and move the phone away from her ear a few inches.

"I knew you had it in ya! Don't forget that I'll be there in a few days."

"I haven't forgotten. You promised to show me the..."

A knock at the door drew her attention and she quickly said goodbye to her friend before pressing the end button and hurrying into the living room. Patting her hair to ensure it was in place, she plastered a smile on her face before swinging the door open. "Ye..." The words died on her lips when she saw the man standing on the other side. "Quinn?"

"It's you?"

Skyler stared up into his piercing blue eyes, so captivated by them that she didn't realize he had spoken until he shifted his stance. Blinking rapidly, she stepped back and waved toward the inside of her room. "Please, come in."

"I... no."

"No?"

"I'm sorry. I think there's been some sort of mistake." Turning on his heel, he took two steps before spinning back around and running a hand nervously through his black hair. "You wouldn't happen to be Sky by any chance?"

"That would be me. Why?"

"Shit." Scrubbing his face vigorously, he looked down at his booted feet and grunted.

"That bad, huh?"

Lifting his head enough to look up at her, he gave her a closed lip smile and shook his head. "Not bad by a long shot, just not what or who I was expecting."

Leaning against the open door, Sky crossed her arms beneath her breasts and cocked her hip to the side. "What exactly were you expecting, Quinn? Someone a little more..."

Lifting a finger to halt her next words, he gave her a steely glare and tsked as he wagged his finger back and forth. "I am to be called Q. Are we clear?"

Returning his glare, she stood from her relaxed position and propped her hands on her hips, her tiny pink tongue darting out as she licked her bottom lip. "Excuse me? Are we clear? Did you really just say that to me?"

A slow smile spread across his face, and he bit down on the corner of his bottom lip as he let his eyes rove over her body before walking forward. "Oh, this is definitely the right cottage."

Skyler pursed her lips and waited for him to get closer before speaking through gritted teeth. "What are you doing here, Quinn?"

"That's one." He advanced on her, forcing her to step further inside the cottage.

"One what? I don't understand what's happening here. Quinn, just stop! Give me a second to process all of this."

His hand dropped to his belt and he smiled when he saw her eyes widen. Releasing the buckle, he advanced on her and quickly pulled the belt through his belt loops. "That's two."

Skyler's eyes followed the movement of the belt as he curled it around his fist. She wasn't stupid. She knew his intentions and the throb between her legs had her opening her mouth and whispering his name again. "Quinn?"

His jaw muscles flexed, and his hand tightened on the belt as he kicked the door shut and pointed toward the back of the sofa. "That's three."

Her legs shook as she turned and walked over to the sofa. Looking back at him, she untied the belt of her robe and let it fall to the floor, biting back a smile when she heard the quick intake of his breath. Bending over the back of the couch, she grasped the cushion in front of her and waited for the kiss of leather against her bare flesh.

She cried out as pain flared through her body when the belt bit into the cheeks of her ass. She knew it would hurt but she craved the pain as much as she craved her next breath. Wiggling her ass, she silently begged him for more and her legs quivered when he delivered another stinging blow.

"Who am I?"

"Quinn." She heard the hiss of the belt through the air and braced herself for the pain. Heat radiated between her thighs, and she knew she was close to an orgasm. Her body jerked when the belt smacked against her flesh, and she buried her face in the cushion as she rolled her hips. His breath was hot against her ear when he spoke, and she wanted to turn to meet his gaze but embarrassment kept her face in the cushion.

"Who am I?"

Lifting her head a fraction of an inch, she drew a breath when he stepped back, and she glanced back at him before uttering his name again. "You are Quinn."

The belt came down on her ass again, harder than before and this time she cried out in ecstasy as she came. She tensed when she felt his hands on the globes of her ass cheeks but relaxed when she realized he was attempting to rub the pain away. His voice was a deep rumble next to her ear again.

"From now on you will call me Q. Any other name will result in punishment. Do you understand?" When she nodded, he squeezed her right ass cheek until she whimpered and asked again. "Do you understand?"

"Ye... yes."

Again, he squeezed her ass cheek. "Yes, what?"

Her body began to tremble, and she fought the desire to press back against his hand. "Yes, sir." She chanced a glance at him from the corner of her eye again and swallowed a moan when she caught him biting down on his lower lip as he stared down at her naked ass. She quickly closed her eyes when she felt him shift his body and remove his hand from her.

"Meet me by the pool later." It was a demand, not an invite, and he waited for her to nod in agreement before turning and walking towards the door.

She lay across the back of the couch, eyes closed, until she heard the cottage door open and close. Lifting her head, she stared into the mirror across the room and a slow smile spread across her lips. Her voice was whisper soft when she spoke to her reflection. "Thank you, Daisy."

Chapter 6

Quinn paced near the edge of the pool, grumbling beneath his breath, as he glanced at his watch. He expected Sky twenty minutes ago and, as the minutes ticked by, he began to plot out her next punishment for keeping him waiting. Hearing feminine laughter behind him, he looked over his shoulder and narrowed his eyes in disapproval. He turned to fully face Sky and folded his hands in front of himself, two fingers tapping slowly over the back of his knuckles. When she finally looked his way, he dipped his head slightly and pointed towards his feet.

Sky's top lip lifted in a sneer of confusion, and she turned back to the woman she had been talking to. "Anyway, so yeah, this is my first time h..." Sky stopped speaking when the woman dropped her head and lowered her gaze to her lap. "Is something wrong?" When the woman remained silent, Sky looked around and finally realized that Quinn was telling her to come to him. "It... it was nice to meet you."

Quinn watched as she casually strolled towards him, her head held high as she attempted to appear unfazed by his silent command. When she stopped in front of him, he narrowed his eyes at her before turning his back to her. Keeping his voice low, he spoke loud enough for her to hear him. "You are never to wear that out in public again."

"I'm sorry... what?"

His shoulders tensed and he flexed his hands to keep from curling them into tight fists. "From now on, you are to get my approval before dressing to appear in public."

Sky's mouth dropped open, and she stared at his broad back for a second before snapping her mouth closed and turning on her heel to walk away. "I'll be damned if I let you or anyone else dictate how I dress."

His hand clamped down on her wrist, effectively halting her. "You don't leave until I grant you permission to leave."

Sky spun to face him and tried to jerk free of his grip as she glared up at the stern expression on his face. "Let go of me, Quinn!"

His jaw flexed at her usage of his name and his nostrils flared as he leaned down close to her ear. "You will be punished when we get back to my cottage. Once for wearing this delectable bikini without my permission. Once for every time you've defied me. Once for thinking of walking away. And once for using my name after I have forbidden it. Nod if you understand."

"Why...?"

Quinn chuckled and shook his head. "I wouldn't speak if I were you." He leaned back enough to see the side of her face. "Do you understand?"

Closing her mouth, she swallowed and looked at him from the corner of her eye. Her nod was slow to come, and she closed her eyes in humiliation as she nodded in understanding.

"Good girl. Now. Go back to your cottage and change into something less revealing, then return here. I have scheduled a tour of the island for us." Releasing his hold on her wrist, he stepped back and waited for her to open her eyes. When she looked up at him, he lifted his chin a notch and indicated the direction she had just came from. "Do not stop or speak to anyone. Go change and come straight back here."

Sky wanted to defy him with every fiber of her being. She hated being told what to do by anyone, much less someone she barely knew. Turning quickly, she hurried from the pool area and gritted her teeth in anger as she waited for an escort to take her back to her cottage.

Chapter 7

"Good afternoon Master Q. I am Leo and I will be your guide for the day." Looking toward Sky, Leo dropped his eyes to the ground and gave a slight bow. "Mistress Sky."

Quinn looked at the man in front of him and sucked his teeth in annoyance when he caught him glancing at Sky's bare feet. "Do we need to have a meeting, Leo?"

Leo's head jerked up and his eyes widened when he noticed the look on Quinn's face. "Sir, I apologize. I meant no disrespect."

Stepping forward, Quinn leaned down until his face was near the man's ear. "I catch you looking again and there will be harsh consequences, do you understand?"

"Ye ... yes, sir. I understand."

"Good." Standing to his full height, Quinn offered his arm to Sky and smiled down at Leo as she linked her arm through his. "Shall we get this tour underway then?"

Clearing his throat, Leo turned away from them and began walking along the tree lined path, speaking loud enough to be heard by the pair behind him, but low enough to avoid drawing unwanted attention. "As you can see, we have a multitude of activities to keep you entertained during your stay. To the right we have..."

Quinn looked down at the woman on his arm and Leo's words faded away when he caught her staring up at him, her eyes large and questioning. "What's wrong?"

Sky looked down at her feet and back up at him before speaking. "What did you whisper to Leo back there?"

Quinn's jaw flexed once, and he turned his attention to the beach. "There are certain rules that must be adhered to, and he broke one of those rules."

"Which was?" His gaze dropped to her face, and she gasped at the anger she saw in his eyes.

"He looked at you without my permission."

Sky stopped walking as her mouth dropped open in disbelief. "What? Why would he need your permission?"

Quinn shook his head at Leo when the man turned to face them. "We'll do the tour another day, Leo. You may go now."

Dipping his head in acknowledgement, Leo turned to the left and disappeared down the path leading away from the beach.

Turning back to face Sky, Quinn dislodged her hold and stepped back so she could look at him without straining her neck. "You don't know anything about this lifestyle, do you?"

"I..." Sky clasped her hands together and popped her knuckles nervously. "I know enough."

Quinn arched and eyebrow and the corner of his mouth twitched as he held back a smile. "Sugar, I have a feeling you don't know nearly enough." Lifting his arm, he placed a finger beneath her chin and lifted her head as he stepped forward, his voice a low husky whisper as he leaned down, his lips hovering above hers. "But I'm more than willing to teach you everything you desire to learn." His tongue flicked out and lightly grazed her bottom lip before he inhaled her scent and straightened back up. "I made reservations for us to attend a social event this evening. You'll find an appropriate... uh... outfit waiting for you back at your cottage along with details of the event. I'll be around to pick you up at around 8:30."

Sky watched him walk away, her fingers trembling as she lay them against her lips.

Sky held up the black silk dress and bit down on the corner of her bottom lip, a soft smile curving the other corner slightly as she rubbed the cool material against her cheek. Reaching down with one hand, she quickly released her towel and lifted the dress over her head, shivering as the silk slid over her skin. Turning towards the mirror, she was admiring the way the dress hugged her curves when her cellphone chirped. Smoothing her hands over her hips, she smiled and picked up her phone, swiping up to open her text messages.

BEN:

Where the fuck are you?

Sky's eyes grew wide, and she quickly glanced up at the contact name before typing out her reply.

SKYLER:

Excuse me? I don't need to explain my whereabouts to you or anyone else. We are done, Ben. We've been done for weeks.

BEN:

I don't know what gave you the impression that we were done, but I expect your ass to be here in the next twenty minutes or I'm coming to get you.

Sky felt her cheeks flush with anger and her hand tightened on the phone. Her fingertips hovered over the phone's keyboard, and she thought about her response before swiping his message away and pulling up her sister's phone number. She chewed the edge of her thumbnail and waited for Sunni to answer. "Come on. Pick up."

"Hey, Sky. What's up?"

Sky ignored the question and spoke in a rush of words. "Are you home? Ben is furious and is threatening to come over there and I don't want you at the house if he shows up there. Where are you?"

"Whoa there, relax. I'm not even in town, much less

at home. Why would he be mad at you? I thought you called it quits with him?"

"I did. Hell, I thought it was mutual. Look, since you're not even in town, I'll just block him and deal with it when I get back. You mind staying with mom until next week?" Sky pulled the phone from her ear and read the new text sent from Ben.

> BEN:
>
> Stop ignoring me, Skyler. Are you coming or not?

Putting the phone back to her ear, she caught Sunni's last few words.

"...long time ago."

"I'm sorry, Sunni. I was distracted by another text and missed what you said."

"I said, I was planning to stay here for the next two weeks anyway, and you should've blocked Ben's ass a long damn time ago. Look, I have to go but we'll talk again soon, yeah? I want to know all about your secret trip."

Sky laughed and shook her head as she stared at her reflection again. "It wouldn't be a secret if I told you, now would it. Have fun, kid and be safe." Pressing the end icon, Sky opened the texts back up and went through the steps to hide any alerts from

Ben before going into her contacts and blocking his number. Looking at the time on the top of her phone, she powered it off and placed it in the drawer of the bedside table before hurrying from the bedroom.

Chapter 8

Quinn gently pulled at the cuffs of his shirt and released a pent up breath before lifting his hand and knocking on the cottage door in front of him. He shifted nervously as he waited for Sky to answer and silently berated himself for being so nervous. *'Calm down, man. She's not going to bite you.'* The thought of her actually biting him made him smile and he looked down at his booted feet.

"Qui... ah... Q. Won't you come in?"

Quinn slowly lifted his head and released a low whistle as he let his eyes travel up her body. "Perfect fit." Nodding his approval, he stepped to the side and held his hand out towards her. "If you're ready to go..."

Glancing down at her bare feet, Sky held up a

finger and turned back into the cottage, her voice shaky as it floated back to him. "Give me a second to put on my heels and I'll be right out."

Leaning his shoulder against the door frame, Quinn put his hands in his pants pockets and crossed his feet at the ankles, nodding in greeting to a couple walking by. Hearing the tapping of heels approaching, he straightened and faced the door just as Sky stepped back into view.

"Sorry, I didn't realize we'd be leaving so soon." Stepping from the cottage, she pulled the door shut and smiled up at Quinn. "I'm so nervous. I'm telling you this because I tend to babble when I get nervous. It's a bad habit that I can't seem to break. Kind of like when I..."

"Sky?"

"Yes?"

"You're babbling." The corners of his lips lifted in a closed mouthed smile as he watched color stain her cheeks.

"Oh, sorry."

"No need to apologize. If you want, I can help you break the habit."

Her eyes grew wide, and she faltered for a second. "Really? You can do that? Oh that would be great. But how will you..." Her words died in her throat as his mouth covered hers in a kiss. She breathed deep through her nose, filling her lungs with his scent. When the kiss ended, she blinked slowly and stared straight ahead as they resumed walking towards the resort restaurant.

Sky stared in wonder at the decor of the restaurant and was lifting her hand to wave at the woman she had met previously at the pool, when Quinn placed his hand over her wrist and brought her hand back down to her side. "What the he...?" Looking up, she noticed the serious look in his eyes before he looked down and back up quickly. Cocking her head to the side, she opened her mouth to speak when he repeated the motion with his eyes. As under-standing dawned on her, she lowered her eyes to the floor as she silently seethed inside. She hated being treated like a child and swore she would tell him as much when they were seated at their table.

"Good evening, Sir. Your table has been set up and we've placed the privacy screen around your section per your request. If you'll both follow me, I will escort you to your table." The host continued to speak as he led the pair across the restaurant. "I've taken the liberty of having a lovely red sent to your table and the chef is working on an appetizer sure to please you both. It's a delicate avocado and crab nap..."

"I don't eat crab or any other type of shellfish." Sky swallowed her groan of mortification and chanced a glance at Quinn, certain he'd be angry that she had spoken. Her shoulders slumped when he nodded at her before speaking to the host.

"The appetizers sound good but maybe we can have something that the lady would enjoy as well." When Sky looked up at him again, he smiled and motioned for her to speak.

"Perhaps we could get some charred bread with ricotta and cherry salsa. Do you have that?"

"Excellent choice, miss. I will have that brought out straight away." Waving his hand to the side, he stepped back and waited for them to be seated before bowing and walking away.

Picking up her napkin, Sky unfolded it and placed it in her lap, smoothing it out as she spoke softly. "I'd like to apologize for being so abrupt with our host. I'm not accustomed to waiting to be allowed to speak."

Quinn chuckled softly and leaned back in his chair, crossing his arms over his massive chest. "It's okay to speak up when something isn't to your liking." He studied her as she nervously rearranged the silverware in front of her. "Maybe we should take this time to get acquainted with each other. Is there anything I should know about you?"

Sky looked up at him without lifting her head and shrugged. "I mean, as pertains to what? My personal life? No, there's nothing you should know about that. I'm sure we'll never see each other again after I leave this weekend, right?" Sky's breath caught in her throat when he bit down on the edge of his bottom lip. She wondered when she'd get to feel his teeth nibbling on her like he was nibbling his lip. Heat flooded her cheeks when his mouth slowly curved up into a teasing smile as if he had heard her thought.

Dipping his head in a slight nod, Quinn let his eyes travel over her face, noting the slight pink stain coloring her cheeks. His gaze landed on her full lips, and he resisted the urge to capture her mouth with his when she bit down nervously on the tip of her tongue. "Invite me back to your cottage."

Sky's eyes widened and she looked up at the server standing next to their table holding their appetizers. She kept silent as their plates were sat in front of them before the server bowed slightly and backed away, disappearing around the privacy screen.

Quinn watched her as she picked up a piece of charred bread before setting it back down. "Invite me back to your cottage, Sky."

Swallowing, Sky laid a hand on her stomach and wondered if she really wanted to wait until the weekend before leaving. "It's... you don't want to get to know each other a bit first?"

Sitting forward, Quinn pushed his plate to the side and propped his elbows on the table before folding his hands together in front of him. "You just said we won't see each other after you leave, so I don't see how getting to know each other is necessary, do you?"

Sky stared at his hands, admiring the length of his fingers, and shifted in her chair when she felt a throb of longing between her legs. "I... I guess not." Taking a deep breath through her nose, she leveled a steady gaze on him and spoke softly but with a hint of authority. "Would you like to come back to my cottage for a bit, Q?"

The smile returned to Quinn's mouth, and he sat back enough to pull his plate back in front of him.

Shrugging, he picked up his own charred toast and took a large bite, wiping his mouth, and swallowing before speaking. "Perhaps. Let's see how dinner goes." He bit back a smile of satisfaction when he heard her sharp intake of breath.

"You bastard. You know what? Fuck it. I don't think you and I being paired is a good idea." Standing, Sky threw her napkin on the table and stomped towards the front of the restaurant, ignoring the sudden whispers and shocked glances from the other guests. Her hand stung as she slammed it against the door, and she curled it into a tight fist as she stepped out into the balmy night.

"Miss?"

"Take me to my cottage."

"But..." Her glare caused the man to step back, and he nodded quickly as he waved towards the nearest escort.

Sky stood beneath the hot spray of water and stared down at her silver painted toenails. She silently berated herself for thinking she could step into this world and walk away unscathed. She had never been one to just fall into bed with a total stranger and she didn't know if she could do it without getting attached. Leaning her head back into the spray of water, she closed her eyes and ran her hands through her hair, her mind made up that she would leave first thing in the morning.

"That was very rude of you."

Her scream reverberated around the tiled walls of the shower, and she quickly covered herself with her hands as she looked up into Quinn's light colored eyes. "What are you doing in my shower? Hell, in my cottage!"

Quinn's hand shot out and stopped inches from her face when she flinched back. Anger bubbled in his stomach and his jaw muscles flexed from gritting his teeth. Slowly reaching towards her again, he cupped her chin in his hand and pulled her forward. "You don't have to be scared of me. I would never strike you out of anger."

"What about the spanking you gave me?"

A smile twitched at the corner of his mouth, and it grew when Sky released a slow sigh of longing. "Aww sugar, that wasn't anger. Soon, you'll know the difference." Lowering his head, he caught her bottom lip between his teeth and lightly nibbled before kissing his way across her jaw and up to her ear. "By the way, you're getting another spanking when you get out of this shower." Catching her earlobe in his mouth, he tugged at her earring until she whimpered. Releasing his hold on her, he stepped from the shower and pulled his belt through the loops of his soaking wet jeans. "I'll be waiting for you in the bedroom. You've got five minutes to meet me there." Quinn was stepping from the bathroom when he stopped and spoke without looking back. "And you're only allowed to touch your pussy enough to wash it, am I clear?" When she didn't answer, he folded the leather belt and snapped it loudly. "Sky? Do you understand?"

Biting down on her bottom lip, Sky closed her eyes and let her head fall back against the shower wall. "Yes, Q. I understand." Her hand trembled as it hovered above her throbbing flesh, and she slowly released a sigh when she heard the click of the door latch falling into place.

Quinn sat in the leather chair and watched the bathroom door as he slowly caressed the belt lying across his knees. He was hard from thinking of all the things he wanted to do to Sky before she left at the end of the week. The sweet pain he would inflict on her, not just because he would enjoy it, but because she would be begging for it, caused a smile to curl the corner of his mouth. He remembered the soft moans she released with each kiss of his belt against her naked ass the last time and he shifted in the chair as he grew harder beneath the zipper of his jeans. "Sky?"

"Y... yes?"

"Why are you standing at the door instead of coming to me?" Quinn's hand tightened on the belt when he heard her snort of defiance.

"I'll be out in a bit."

"You'll come out now. Don't make me come in there to get you."

"Or what?"

Getting to his feet, Quinn let the belt dangle at his side as he approached the door and laid his free hand against the wood. His words were a deep rumbled whisper, and he knew from experience the reaction they would cause in her body. "Are you sure you're ready for the answer to that question, brat?"

"I am not a brat!"

"Oh, but you are. You are purposely defying me, knowing full well what your punishment will be." He heard the slide of her naked body against the door and smiled when her soft moan reached his ears.

"And if I don't consider it to be punishment?"

Sky moaned again, louder this time, and Quinn's eyes widened with understanding. "I told you to keep your hands to yourself!" Her throaty laughter caused him to tremble with need, and he wrapped his hand around the doorknob.

"But Q, I *am* keeping my hands to myself."

Lifting the belt, he folded it in half before running the folded edge over the wood of the door. "Are you touching yourself, Sky?" He sucked in a deep breath through his teeth when she replied.

"Mmm... and if I am?"

"You're being a very bad girl, Sky. Do you want to be punished?" He heard her shift on the other side of the door and waited a few minutes before turning the doorknob and stepping into the steam filled room. A growl rumbled from his throat when his eyes found her through the steam, her hands wrapped around the towel bar and her beautiful ass arched high in his direction. He licked the corner of his top lip slowly as he stepped in her direction. "Is that a yes then?" He smiled when she nodded and drew his arm back. His moan of pleasure matched hers as the leather folded around her bare ass cheeks and she lifted up on her tiptoes offering him a view of the folds between her legs. He ached to taste her, to make her scream as his tongue delved deep into her pussy, to wring the very essence from her body. Stepping closer, he rubbed his hand over the globes of her red ass and leaned down to whisper in her ear. "Did you disobey me and touch yourself after I told you not to?"

Sky turned her head enough to look at him from over her shoulder. "Yes." Her eyes widened when he quickly stepped back and brought the belt down across her bare flesh again, a little harder than the last time. Heat flooded her lower stomach, and she wriggled her hips, a silent invitation for more.

Quinn pulled his arm back and rubbed her ass again before bringing the belt back down, enjoying the sound of leather meeting flesh. "Have you had enough? Are you ready to obey?" His eyes narrowed when he caught the slightest sound of her snort of amusement. "You're going to defy me every chance you get, aren't you?" He swallowed back a smile when she turned her head towards him, her eyes hooded with passion, but a smirk playing across her full lips.

"Every chance I get." She shuddered when he brought the belt down one last time.

Grabbing a fistful of her hair, he pulled her head back and bent over until his lips were inches from her own. "You never answered my question, Sky. Are you ready to obey?" Sky's tongue slowly moved across her bottom lip, and he wanted to capture it between his teeth.

"And if I'm not?" Her nostrils flared and she lifted up on her toes when he cupped her from behind.

"The belt is meant to be punishment, but you enjoy it entirely too much." Releasing her, he stepped back and began running the belt back through his belt loops. Keeping his gaze on the floor, he spoke softly but with authority. "Tomorrow night I am taking you across the bay. We have things to work out before we go any further."

"Things? What sort of things?"

Lifting his head, he watched her pull on a silk robe and waited until she had her belt tied before answering. "We will discuss that tomorrow night. In the meantime, I want you to think off for me." The corner of his mouth curved up when Sky's eyebrow arched up in confusion.

"Think off? What does that mean?"

Stepping forward, he grasped the belt of her robe and untied it before pulling it free of the robe. "Turn around." After a brief hesitation, Sky turned, and he tapped her arms with his forefingers. "Behind you." When her hands appeared behind her back, he quickly tied them together with the robe belt before guiding her into the bedroom and over to the vanity. "Sit."

"I'd rather stand."

"Trust me, little one, you'll want to sit." Quinn held onto her arm and waited for her to be seated before kneeling in front of her and pushing her legs wide.

"Qui... Q?"

"Close your eyes. Good girl. Now, I want you to tell me what you want me to do right now." Her silence spoke volumes and he slowly ran the side of his hand across her upper thigh causing a moan of longing to escape from her. "What do you desire?"

"I want... I want your mouth on me."

Lifting his hand, Quinn sat back and watched her face, biting his bottom lip when her tongue darted out from her mouth to glide over her lips.

"Can you feel my mouth kissing your thighs? My teeth nibbling a path upwards? The heat of my breath blowing across your pussy causing your curls to move ever so slightly? Can you feel it, Sky?" Quinn's hands shot out and captured her knees when she tried to close her legs. "Leave them open. I want to see you come for me."

"I ca... I can't with you watching."

"You can and you will." Quinn caressed the back of her bent knees and gritted his teeth when she moaned softly. "Open your eyes, look at me." Her eyes cracked open, and she lowered her head to meet his gaze. "Come for me, Sky. Feel my tongue caressing your clit ever so slowly. My hands cupping your ass to hold you still as I lick my way down, nibbling at your tender flesh along the way. Feel my tongue as I press it against your..." He smiled when she gasped and let his gaze fall to the curls between her legs. Gripping her knees, he pushed her legs wider, and licked his bottom lip, the urge to taste her release almost more than he could stand. Lifting his head, he met her smoldering gaze and dipped his head in a slight nod. "Good girl." Sitting back, he released his hold on her knees and got to his feet to walk behind her. She shivered when he trailed his fingers down her arms to the robe belt tied around her wrists. Giving the end of the belt a tug, he let it fall to the floor as he stepped back in front of Sky and helped her to her feet before picking her up and carrying her to the bed. "Rest now. In a bit, I want you to get up and eat. Don't forget to drink plenty of water as well."

"I ..."

Quinn arched an eyebrow and her mouth snapped closed as she nodded and rolled to her side. "I'll be by tomorrow morning to pick you up. Be ready and dress comfortably. We will be swimming. You can bring a suit or don't, I'll leave the decision up to you."

"You're actually going to let me make a decision? Fantastic."

She smirked up at him and Quinn shook his head as he stood straight. "Brat." Turning he left the room and was opening the cottage door to leave when her soft words reached his ears causing him to chuckle.

"I'm not a brat."

Stepping from the cottage, he pulled the door closed and started down the path towards his own cottage, his mind occupied with thoughts of plans for tomorrow.

Chapter 9

Sky stared down at the small box and read the handwritten note that she held between her index finger and middle finger.

You will wear this for the remainder of your stay. See you soon, Q

Lifting the lid of the box, she stared down at the silver necklace and scowled at the word dangling on a thin chain from the Q initial. Lifting her eyes, she met the amused gaze of her friend and pursed her lips in annoyance.

"You don't like it?"

"I'm not sure I have a choice of liking it."

Daisy laughed softly and took a sip of her

cappuccino before answering. "Of course you have a choice."

"But I still have to wear it." Sky traced the word with her fingertip before looking up at Daisy when she heard the other woman's soft chuckle.

"But you still have to wear it."

The necklace was cool against her fingertips, and she wrapped her fingers around the brat pendent, her emotions racing from anger to excitement as she stared at Daisy's amused expression. "What would happen if I don't wear it?" Opening her hand, she stared down at the silver Q and huffed out a disbelieving chuckle. "I bet he has a shit ton of these that he doles out to his playthings regularly."

Putting her cup down, Daisy waited for her to look at her again before speaking. "If your guy is who I suspect he is, he doesn't give jewelry to just anyone. He's not the sort to toy with his partner's emotions like that. He has his reasons for marking you."

"Marking me? You can't be serious right now? I'm not his possession."

"Relax. It's not as bad as it sounds. And, in a few days, you can give it back if you don't want to keep it."

Sky watched her friend for a few minutes before

closing the lid on the jewelry box and turning towards the bedroom. "I need to finish getting ready. Q is supposed to be here sometime this morning to pick me up."

Following Sky into the room, Daisy walked over to the bed and stretched out across it, resting her chin on her crossed arms as she watched Sky push clothes around in the wardrobe. "Anything in particular he wants you to wear?"

Sky shook her head and held a wispy sundress against her body as she turned toward the mirror. "He said to dress comfortably. What do you think of this?"

Daisy stared at the dress and nodded. "That's cute, but maybe it's a little too fancy for a day on the beach? Do you have a romper or something less dressy?"

Turning back to look inside the wardrobe she pulled out a white strappy back jumpsuit. "Like this?"

Daisy smiled. "Exactly like that. Go try it on and let me see how it looks."

Sky was walking toward the bathroom when she stopped and turned towards her friend. "He gave me the choice of wearing a bikini or swimming in the nude. I think he may be testing me and well..." Dropping the robe to the floor, Sky stepped into the jumpsuit and pulled the top up over her chest before turning to present her back to Daisy. "You mind tying this for me?"

Sitting up, Daisy let her eyes travel the length of Sky's body before clearing her throat and speaking. "Uh... Sky, I can see your, well... everything. Are you sure you want to wear this without a bikini or even a thong beneath it?"

Looking over her shoulder, Sky gave Daisy a wicked smile as she arched an eyebrow. "What's he going to do, spank me?"

"You do realize there's more ways he can punish you besides spanking, right?" Daisy was reaching for the ties of the jumpsuit when a knock sounded from the front of the cottage.

Sky's eyes widened and she looked towards the bedroom door when the knock came again, more persistent than the last. "Would you mind answering that for me while I finished getting ready?"

Daisy gave a brisk nod before hurrying from the room.

As the door closed behind her friend, Sky pulled the jumpsuit back off and quickly pulled a pair of lacy thongs from the top drawer of the dresser.

The smile fell from Daisy's face when she opened the door, and she averted her gaze. "Sir. Sky is still getting ready. Won't you come in?"

Quinn's voice held a hint of amusement when he spoke. "Little Flower. I didn't expect to see you this season." Stepping forward, he placed a knuckle beneath her chin and lifted her head so he could look into her eyes. "Are you joining us then?"

Daisy held her breath as she stared up into his beautiful ice blue eyes and slightly shook her head. "N... no sir."

"Too bad. Maybe next time." Dropping his hand, he stepped around her and walked towards Sky's room.

Daisy shut the door and hesitated before hurrying after him. "Can I get you something to drink while we wait for Sky in the living room?"

Quinn ignored her question and continued towards the bedroom. "You may leave us, Little Flower."

"But, sir, I..." Her words died in her throat when

he cast a disapproving look at her over his shoulder. Her steps faltered and she once again dropped her gaze. "Yes, sir." Turning she made her way back down the hall and out the front door, her breath leaving her in a rush as she sprinted down the pathway towards her own cottage, tears of shame, anger, and regret coursing down her cheeks. She thought she knew who had sent Sky the necklace, but she had been wrong. She stumbled as she looked back over her shoulder, her tears falling faster and her need to do something to stop Sky from leaving with the man she had just spoken to growing stronger. She never would've told Sky about the resort had she known there was a chance of her being paired up with *the Raven*.

Chapter 10

Sky held onto her sun hat with one hand and gripped the railing of the tiny boat with the other, her eyes squinted against the salt water spraying her face, as they raced across the bay.

"Sky?"

Hearing her name, she turned and smiled at Quinn. "Did you say something?"

Quinn arched an eyebrow before lifting his hand and motioning her over. "Come stand next to me."

Sky shook her head, her eyes wide with fright. "I don't think that's a good idea, Q."

His face darkened with displeasure as he snapped his fingers and pointed to the spot beside him. "Sky. Now."

Sky stared at him, stunned by what had just

happened. "Excuse me? Did you just command me as if I were a dog?" Her grip on the railing tightened when the boats speed abruptly decreased.

"You're disobeying me?"

"And you're treating me like a dog." Her body swayed towards him when he brought the boat to a stop, and she laid a hand on her stomach to keep from being sick.

Quinn noticed the way she began to swallow repeatedly, and his displeasure turned to concern. "Are you all right? You look like yo..." His words cut off in a grimace when she turned and leaned over the side of the boat. Stepping up beside her, he pulled her hair back over her shoulder and rubbed her back as she emptied the contents of her stomach over the side of the boat. "Why didn't you tell me you were sick?"

Sky lay her sweaty forehead against her arm and silently wished she were invisible. "Because I wasn't sick when you picked me up. I'm sorry you have to be a witness to this."

"No need to apologize... well, not about being sick that is."

Sky turned a glare in his direction and tried to pull her hair free of his grasp. "I have nothing to apologize for then because I'm not sorry for what I said."

His hand tightened in her hair, and he gritted his teeth as he smiled and leaned down next to her face, his breath causing her to shiver as he whispered into her ear. "You will regret defying me, brat." Releasing her hair, he tugged on the brat pendent hanging from her necklace before returning to the helm of the boat.

Quinn looked at his watch before holding his hand out towards Sky. "Come with me."

Sky opened her mouth to protest but, seeing the look in his eyes, sighed and stood up from the lounge chair. "Are we going to get lunch soon?"

Quinn smiled softly and nodded. "Soon, but not yet."

Taking his outstretched hand, Sky allowed Quinn to lead her down a sandy path, her eyes darting left to right as she tried to locate the source of music she was hearing. "What is that? I thought we were alone?"

Quinn ignored her and turned off the path, pulling her after him as he walked through the trees, his stride quickening as the music grew louder.

Sky ran into his back when he suddenly stopped walking. Her body instantly reacted when she pressed against him, and heat flooded her face as her nipples grew hard against his naked flesh. Dropping her gaze, she tried to tug her hand free of his hold. "Sorry."

Tightening his grip, Quinn tugged her forward and stepped behind her, his arm appearing over her shoulder as he pointed. "Watch."

Sky leaned away and looked over her shoulder at him in confusion. "Watch?" Cutting her eyes in the direction he was pointing, she shook her head and looked back at him. "There's nothing there, Q."

Laying his hand against her throat, he caressed her flushed skin before moving his hand up and catching her chin in the crook between his thumb and forefinger. He stared at her lips and clenched his teeth when her tongue darted from her mouth as she licked her bottom lip, as if anticipating the feel of his mouth pressed against hers. Applying firm pressure to her chin, he turned her head back in the direction he had pointed earlier and leaned down close to her ear. "Wait and watch."

Sky shivered in need and balled her hands into fists at her side to keep from reaching back for him. "I don't see..." Her words trailed off when a masked woman stepped into view followed closely by a man wearing a mask as well. Both were naked and the man was visibly aroused. Sky tried to look away when the woman dropped to her knees in front of the man.

"No. Watch."

"But I... this feels so wrong. They ..."

"They both know someone is watching."

Sky shifted slightly when the woman looked over her shoulder in their direction before lifting up on her knees, spreading her legs wide, and leaning forward, her bare pussy slick with desire as her fingers toyed with her clit. "But not who? They don't know it's us?"

Quinn's breath touched her neck as he spoke, and his hands fell to her hips. "They don't care who watches as long as someone does."

Sky pressed her ass back against Quinn and sucked in a sharp breath when the masked woman turned on her knees and presented the man with her naked ass, her voice husky as it drifted to Sky's ears.

"Fuck me... now. And don't be gentle."

Sky reached back to untie her jumpsuit, but

Quinn caught her hand and pulled it away before grasping her other wrist and forcing her hands to her side. "You will watch, that is all."

Sky whimpered in need as the man in front of her thrust his cock deep inside the woman, his neck muscles straining as she ground herself against him.

Quinn let his hands travel around Sky's waist and down to her inner thighs. "Spread your legs for me, brat."

Sky parted her legs and bit down on her bottom lip as she waited for him to move his hands higher. When he didn't, she bent her knees and rocked her hips forward, biting back a squeak of pain when he pinched her thigh.

"Be still, brat." When she whimpered again, he kissed her neck lightly before whispering in her ear. "Remember when I told you you'd regret defying me?"

Sky was nodding when she felt his hand close over her. Heat flooded her core and she tried to close her legs to trap his hand, crying out when he moved it away.

"No no, little brat. You don't come until I tell you to. Are we clear?" When Sky nodded, Quinn trailed his hands over the front of her body as he stepped around her and stared down into her eyes. "Do you want to keep watching?"

Sky wanted to say no but, hearing the cries of passion from the masked woman, she bit down on the corner of her bottom lip and nodded. Her eyes widened when Quinn dropped to his knees in front of her and she looked down at him.

Quinn pointed up at her. "Don't watch me. Watch them."

Sky's heart thundered in her chest as she lifted her head and looked towards the couple. The woman was now straddling the masked man, her ass pointed in their direction offering Sky of view of the man's cock driving into the woman as she rode him hard. Sky lifted her leg when Quinn patted it and resisted the urge to look down when he worked her foot through the split in the leg of her jumpsuit. She moaned when he nipped the inside of her thigh twice before covering her bare flesh with his mouth. When she felt the first flick of his tongue against her clit, all self-control shattered and she buried her fingers in his hair, pressing him closer as she ground herself against his mouth. Her eyes rolled back as she rode the waves of ecstasy, pumping her hips faster as she raced towards release. When she felt Quinn's hands on her wrists, her eyes flew open, and she pulled her hands free. Her eyes were wide with shock over what she had done and she covered her mouth when Quinn pulled away and looked up at her, his eyes shining with amusement. "I'm sorry."

"I said not to come until I told you to."

Sky held up her hands, her eyes wide as she struggled to speak. "I mean…" Waving towards the couple she shrugged. "I couldn't help it."

Quinn licked his lips before slowly standing to cup her face. "Looks like we need to work on your self-control, brat."

Sky nodded in agreement and swayed towards him, attempting to capture his mouth in a kiss.

Quinn pulled his head away and smirked at her. "I couldn't stop you from coming but I can keep you from taking the pleasure you seek in my mouth."

"Couldn't or didn't want to?" She squeaked out a laugh when Quinn swatted her ass cheek before kneeling in front of her again and running his hand down her calve.

"Lift your foot for me."

She shivered in anticipation and did as she was told. As if sensing her thoughts, Quinn chuckled and lightly kissed her inner thigh before he slipped her leg back inside her jumpsuit. She stared down at his dark head and silently berated herself for the way her heartbeat quickened. When he patted her leg, she stepped back and waited for him to stand before looking back in the direction where the couple had been. "They've left?"

Following the direction of her gaze, Quinn nodded before taking her hand in his and guiding her back toward the path that led to the beach. "They got what they came for. Are you hungry?"

Sky nodded and looked down at her feet when her stomach answered for her. "I could eat."

Quinn's laughter filled the air, and he squeezed her fingers briefly as they stepped back out onto the beach.

Chapter 11

Sky was drying her hair when a knock came from the front of the cottage. Stepping into her bedroom, she noted the late hour and her brow furrowed as she made her way into the living room. Holding the towel to her chest, she moved the peephole cover to the side before looking out. Shaking her head, she took a deep calming breath before stepping to the side and pulling the door open. "Daisy? Is everything all right?" Her gaze fell to the tote bag that Daisy had clutched in her fists. "Are you..."

"I was told to come visit you."

Confusion drew Sky's brow down and she looked out into the night, expecting to see Quinn standing behind her friend. "Excuse me? Who told you to visit me?"

Instead of answering, Daisy handed Sky a folded piece of paper and stepped inside the cottage.

Sky looked at Daisy's back as the other woman walked over to the couch and sat the tote at her feet. "Well, please, come on in and make yourself at home." Closing the door, she looked down at the piece of paper and flicked it open, her eyes darting over the typed words as she reread them for the third time. "What the fuck does this mean, Daisy? How do you know Q?"

Daisy spun to face Sky and she shook her head. "That's just it. I don't know him. I've heard of him, I've seen him from afar, hell I've been warned to stay far away from him. But I don't *know* him."

"Then what's this *Little Flower* shit? And why does he think I... You're my friend, Daisy. That's all."

"I heard you?"

Sky's brow drew down in confusion and she crossed her arms over her chest as she began tapping her foot in annoyance. "I'm sure I don't know what you're talking about."

"Cut the shit, Skyler. I heard you. I know it was you that watched me today. Did you like what you saw? Did it make you come?"

Sky's head snapped up and she stared into Daisy's eyes as her friend slowly approached her.

"That was …. you? Why didn't you say anything if you knew I was the one watching? I never would've…" When Daisy smiled seductively at her, Sky held up a hand. "Wait. What do you want from me, Daisy?"

"I'm only following a command." Daisy stopped in front of Sky and lifted her hand to loop her finger in the front of the towel that was wrapped around Sky's naked torso.

Sky's heart began to race, and she clinched her teeth when Daisy tugged on the towel. Holding the towel tighter in her clenched fist, she stepped back and shook her head. "You don't have to do this." Her breath hitched in her throat when Daisy leaned forward and kissed the top of her breast. "Daisy, I…"

Daisy looked up and kissed her way up to Sky's neck. "Do you want me to stop? All you have to do is tell me to stop."

Sky sucked in her breath as Daisy's fingers trailed up her inner thigh. "I've never bee…" The words lodged in her throat, and she clutched Daisy's wrist to keep her from going any higher. "Daisy, stop." Backing away from her friend, Sky shook her head again before turning and running towards the bedroom. Once inside, she closed the door and leaned back against it, her heart racing as her mind spun with confusion and anger.

"Sky, please don't be mad at me I..."

"Just go, Daisy. I'll talk to you tomorrow or something. But right now, I need you to just go away." Lowering her hand to rest against the doorknob, Sky silently twisted the door lock and stepped away from the door. "I don't know why Q sent you here, but I really need you to leave."

"But Sky..."

"Just go!" Hurrying across the room, Sky fumbled through the papers lying on the bedside table and picked up her cellphone when she found the one she was looking for. Pressing the number in on the keypad, she hugged herself tightly as she waited for the other person to answer. As soon as she heard the ringing end she began speaking in a rush. "How could you do that to me? She's my friend, my best friend and you send her over? For what? So you can get off knowing we fucked? Just tell me why? Why her?"

"Whoa, slow down there, brat. What the hell are you talking about?"

"I saw the note, Quinn!"

"What note?"

"Don't act like you don't know what I'm talking

about. The note! The fucking note you sent to Daisy telling her to pay me a visit." Sky swiped at her cheek and scowled down at her hand, wet with her tears of anger. "I'm done. I can't do this. I thought I could, but I can't. I'm going home."

"Sky, just calm down. I honestly have no idea what note you're referring to. That necklace you're wearing, that's telling others to keep their hands off. If I wanted to keep you to myself, why would I send Daisy over there to keep you company? Do you still have the note?"

Sky shook her head and looked toward the locked door. "I don't... I'm not sure."

"What do you mean, you're not sure?"

"I ran, okay? I ran like a scared little bitch and locked myself in my room." Sky sucked in her breath and walked backwards until her back was pressed against the wall. "Someone's out there."

"I know. It's me. Are you dressed?"

"N... no."

"Get dressed and come out here so we can talk."

Before Sky could reply she heard three beeps letting her know the call had been disconnected. Going into the bathroom, she pulled on her pajama's before looking at herself in the mirror. Her eyes fell to the necklace still latched around her neck and she wondered if maybe Quinn was telling the truth about the note. If he hadn't sent Daisy over, who did? A soft tapping on the bedroom door pulled her attention away from the necklace and she hurried across the room to open the door. Her fingers touched the lock and she hesitated, uncertain if it was Quinn standing on the other side. "Quinn?"

"That's two, brat."

Rolling her eyes, she twisted the locked and eased the door open. "Those don't count. I was angry."

Leaning down, he lightly kissed her bottom lip, his breath hot against her mouth when he whispered. "They count." Standing back up, Quinn held up his hand, the note tucked between two fingers. "Found this on the floor near the door. I don't know what's going on, but I didn't write this."

"Do you not call Daisy Little Flower?"

"Yeah, because that's the name she goes by when she visits. And I'm telling you, I didn't write this note." Quinn turned and started from the room, his back stiff as he slid the note in the front pocket of his black slacks. "There's a bag in here that I'm assuming belongs to Little Flower."

Hurrying to catch up to him, Sky clutched his

arm and pulled him to a stop. "Have you been with her?"

"I really don't see how that's any of your business, brat."

Sky swallowed down the hurt his words caused and quickly reminded herself that he was nothing to her except a brief encounter. Dropping her hand, she sniffed and lifted her chin a notch. "You're right, it isn't any of my business who you've been with." Reaching up, she began to remove the necklace he had given her.

"Leave it on." When she looked at him, her mouth tight with defiance, he grabbed her wrist and jerked her against his body. Cupping the back of her head, he tightened his fingers in her hair and pulled her head back until he was staring down into her angry eyes. "I said to leave it on, brat."

Sky's words were low and dangerous when she spoke through gritted teeth. "I'm not your brat. Now let me go."

"No. You're being a very bad girl, Sky."

"Yeah? Well I'm about to be downright naughty if you don't get your fucking hands off of me, Quinn." As soon as she said the words she longed to call them back. This close to him, she couldn't miss the reaction those words had on the man holding her against his body. Heat flooded her lower stomach, and she squeezed her thighs together as she dropped her gaze. "I didn't mean..."

Quinn's mouth turned up at the corners and he dropped his hand to Sky's ass and pulled her tighter against his groin. "That's three, brat."

Sky bit back a squeal of surprise when Quinn picked her up and wrapped her legs around his waist. She opened her mouth to speak but he swallowed her words as he fused his mouth to hers. Sky's eyes rolled back in her head, and she buried her hands in his hair to hold his mouth to hers when he tried to pull back. Her tongue delved deep, and she locked her ankles together and lifted herself slightly until she felt the tip of his cock through his slacks.

Quinn groaned beneath Sky's mouth as she rubbed herself against the outside of his slacks, her kiss growing deeper as she sought release. Reaching back, he pried her ankles apart and forced her to release her tight hold on his waist. Turning his head, he broke their kiss and rested his forehead against hers, panting and trying to regain control of the situation. Feeling Sky tremble against his chest, he cursed silently and scooped her up in his arms. Turning back to the bedroom, he carried her inside and kicked the door closed before laying her on the foot of the bed. His hand rested on her exposed stomach for a minute as he watched her worry her bottom lip with her teeth. Growling low in his throat, he jerked her slick sleep shorts down her legs and dropped to his knees in front of her.

Sky parted her legs as she looked down her body at him. "Taste me."

Quinn shook his head. "You don't give the orders."

Lifting up on her elbows, Sky narrowed her eyes at him and repeated her command. "Taste me." Lifting her head a bit, she gave him a saucy smile and rocked her hips. "Come on, Q. Fuck me with your mouth. Do the things to me that you desire so much."

"Careful, brat. You don't want me to do all the things to you that I desire." His gaze dropped when she shifted her weight and spread her legs wider. "You're asking for trouble, brat."

"Then give me trouble."

His head shot up and he arched a dark brow. "If I fuck you, it won't be with my mouth. Is that what you want? Do you want me to bury my cock so deep in your pussy that you won't know where I end, and you begin? Is that what you want from me, brat?"

Sky bit down on the corner of her bottom lip and shrugged. "I..."

"Yes or no, brat? It's a simple answer." Lowering his hand, he released the button of his slacks and slowly drew down the zipper. "I can give you whatever you want, all you need to do is ask." When she opened her mouth to speak, he held up a finger to stop her. "Ask, not demand."

Color flooded her cheeks, and she turned her head away and spoke in a soft whisper. "I can't ask."

"But you can. Look at me and tell me what you want, Sky."

Sky shook her head and tried to close her legs. Her breath left her in a rush when she felt Quinn's hands grip her knees. Looking up at him again, she shook her head. "I can't ask. It's embarrassing asking a man to... to lick me... umm... there."

Quinn's eyes widened as realization hit him. Leaning down over her, he cupped her chin lightly and held her head still so she wouldn't turn away again. "Say it, Sky."

Sky licked her bottom lip and tried to turn her head. "S... say what?"

"You know what I'm talking about. Say it." When her tongue darted out again, he captured it between his teeth before gently sucking on it and releasing it with a slight nip. "Say it. Tell me where exactly you want me to lick you."

Instead of answering him, Sky moved her hips against his erection and tried to capture his mouth in a kiss.

Leaning away, Quinn pressed his palm against her lower stomach and pushed her hips back to the bed. "Nuh uh... not until you say it."

"You're an evil man."

Leaning down next to her ear, Quinn caught her earlobe between his teeth and nibbled briefly before releasing it. His breath was hot against her ear when he spoke in a low deep whisper. "Pussy. Say it."

Sky pressed her naked ass against the bed as a throb began between her legs. "No. I can't." Her nipples hardened and she shivered when he spoke again, the word ending on a growl.

"Pussy."

Her heart pounded and she lay back against the bed as she placed her hands against his waist, whimpering as she tried to pull him down on top of her. "Please, Q... please. I need... I need..."

Quinn stood up and lifted her hips, holding her tightly as he ground his hardened cock against her heat. "What do you need, Sky?"

A moan escaped her, and she squeezed her eyes

shut tightly as she felt herself nearing release. Her body felt like it was burning up and a delicious tingle began in her lower stomach. A smile was forming on her lips, and she cried out in dismay when Quinn released her hips and her ass fell back to the bed. Her eyes flew open, and she stared up at him in bewilderment. "What's wrong?"

"I didn't tell you that you could come."

Shock caused her eyes to widen, and she was opening her mouth to argue when he cupped her and pressed down on her clit with his thumb. "Q..."

"You don't come until I tell you to, and I won't tell you to until you say it."

Sky rolled her head from side to side and licked her suddenly dry lips. "I can't say it, Q. I just can't." Her hips jerked when he pressed down on her clit again and she ached to feel him buried deep inside her.

"Say it." Quinn moved his thumb over her clit and smile as he watched the word form on her lips.

"Pu..."

Inserting a finger into her heat, he curled it and worked it in and out, enjoying the feel of her muscles growing tighter. "Say it, brat. I know you can."

Sky felt Quinn's grip on her hips relax enough

for her to move and she began to quickly rock her hips, riding his finger as she searched for release. When she felt his finger uncurl, she grabbed his wrist to hold him inside and she stared up into his eyes, her eyes hot with desire. "Pussy."

Quinn jerked his hand away from her grip and let her fall back to the bed before dropping to his knees and burying his face between her legs. She was hot against his tongue, and he licked her twice before drawing her bud into his mouth. He hummed against her swollen flesh and chuckled as he felt her fingers curl in his hair. He didn't try to stop her when she pushed his head lower and began riding his tongue.

"Now? Q... please... now."

He answered her with a primal growl as he thrust his tongue inside her, catching her essence on his tongue as she finally cried out with her release.

Chapter 12

Quinn stared across the table at the woman sitting on the opposite side and drummed his fingers impatiently. "I'm waiting, Little Flower."

Daisy nervously twisted her fingers in her lap and chewed her inner cheek as she avoided looking Quinn in the eyes. "Like I told Sky, I was following a command. Which, to be fair, I thought was issued by you."

Quinn rapped his knuckles on the table and waved the waiter over when he caught his eye. "Bring me a scotch and the lady will have..."

"The same."

Quinn's eyebrows lifted and he leaned forward slightly. "Why are you pretending to be shy, Little Flower? We both know that's not your style."

Daisy finally looked at Quinn and pursed her lips in thought. Making up her mind, she sat back and crossed her arms beneath her breasts. "Did you know people call you the *Raven*? You scare the shit out of most of the regulars here and I've been warned to stay away from you. And now, now my best friend is your sub." Quinn's sharp burst of laughter stopped her from continuing. "Did I say something funny?"

"Sky is no one's sub." Lowering his gaze, he pushed his tongue against his inner cheek as he remembered the taste of her from the night before. When the waiter brought their drinks to the table, Quinn took a sip of the Scotch before speaking again. "Back to why I asked you here. Where did you get this note?"

"It was in my room when I returned from across the bay. I admit that I found it a bit odd but figured if you had her watch me being fucked, you'd probably have me go to her cottage." Daisy took a sip of her own drink and studied his face for signs of anger. "Why did you have her watch me and not someone else?"

"I didn't bring her there to specifically watch you. I didn't know beforehand who we would be watching. You know that's not how it works."

"But you didn't leave once you saw that it was me. Why?"

Quinn cocked his head to the side and looked towards the window facing the beach. "My reasons are no concern of yours."

"They are when it involves me."

"You're an exhibitionist, are you not?"

Daisy rolled her eyes and took a healthy swig from her glass, wincing as the Scotch burned its way down her throat.

"Burns a bit, doesn't it?"

Daisy lifted her middle finger without thinking but quickly lowered her hand when she noticed the disapproving arch of his eyebrow. "Why do they call you *the Raven*?"

Quinn lifted his hand in a dismissive gesture and smiled as if amused. "I wasn't aware that they did until you told me just now. Tell me... what else do 'they' say about me?"

Daisy opened her mouth to respond but snapped it shut when she noticed Sky walking towards them.

Quinn noticed the change in her attitude and turned his head slowly to look over his shoulder. Seeing Sky approaching their table, he got to his feet and pulled out the chair next to his. "Sky, I didn't know you'd be joining us today."

Sky's brow drew down in confusion and she looked from him to Daisy and back again. "Am I interrupting something?"

Daisy quickly shook her head and motioned for Sky to sit. "No. Nothing at all. We were just having a friendly little chat, right Sir?"

Quinn waited until Sky was seated before returning to his own chair and answering. "I was trying to get to the bottom of Little Flower's visit with you."

Sky's cheeks instantly reddened at the mention of the encounter, and she began to push her chair away from the table. "I'll leave you to it then. I'll just get..."

Quinn grasped her wrist and held her in place when she would have stood up. "Nonsense. There's no need for you to eat alone. This discussion can wait a little longer now that you both know it wasn't me that sent the note."

Sky looked over at Daisy in time to see her nod in agreement. "If you're sure then?"

Lifting his arm, Quinn motioned for the waiter again and inclined his head toward Sky when the young man approached their table.

"What can I get you this afternoon, mistress?"

Sky smiled up and spoke softly. "Can I get a cheeseburger, fries, and a coke?"

The waiter lifted his gaze to meet Quinn's over Sky's head.

Seeing the exchange, Sky turned her attention to Quinn and arched one delicate eyebrow. "Is there a reason he's looking to you for, what I can only assume is, permission to take my order?"

Quinn chuckled at the look on Daisy's face and pointed at Sky. "Told you she's no one's sub."

As the waiter walked away from the table, Sky sat back and crossed her arms beneath her breasts, her eyes narrowed as she studied the look on Daisy's face. "Care to tell me why you're so shocked that I won't kneel to Q?"

Daisy slowly shook her head and took another sip of Scotch. "You have no idea who he is, do you?"

Licking her lips, Sky cast a playful look in Quinn's direction and sat forward to prop her elbows on the table, linking her fingers together and smiling sweetly. "I think I've learned a lot about who he is in the short amount of time I've been here."

"And you still speak to him that way?"

"What way would that be?"

"Defiantly. Disrespectfully. As if you're trying to..." Daisy's eyes dropped to the pendent nestled against Sky's cleavage and she closed her eyes as she dropped her head into her hand. "Brat." Sitting back in her chair, she shook her head when Quinn and Sky began to laugh, their fingers linking on the table as if they had been together for years and she made a mental note to speak to Shade when she returned to her cottage.

Chapter 13

Sky rolled over onto her back and watched Quinn walk into the ocean, his bare skin glistening where the water touched. They had decided to come to the beach to relax after finally going on their tour of the island and Sky had been forcing herself to stay awake as she had lain there, eye's closed, listening to Quinn's soft singing. Watching him now, she chewed on her bottom lip and wondered if she should join him. She knew he was naked, and she didn't know if she'd be able to resist her desire to feel him buried within her much longer. Her breath caught in her throat as he sank beneath the surface of the water and came back up, his muscles flexing as he ran his fingers through his hair. When he looked towards her and winked, she knew he was silently challenging her. Shaking her head, she turned away slightly but watched him from the corner of her eye as he began walking in her direction.

"Come swim with me, brat."

Lowering her eyes a bit, she cleared her throat before speaking. "I don't have a suit, sir." His laughter rippled over her like a delicate touch, and she shivered as it grew closer.

"I don't have a suit either, brat. Come join me anyway."

Turning her head to look at him fully, she released a long appreciative whistle as she took in his nakedness. "Fucking hell." She watched as he lengthened beneath her gaze, and she stood to walk over to him.

"So that's a yes then?"

"Wha...? Huh?"

Placing a crooked knuckle beneath her chin, he pushed her head up until she was looking into his eyes. "You're joining me for a swim." Sky started to shake her head, but he stopped it with a thumb press beneath her bottom lip. "That wasn't a question." Reaching behind her neck, he tugged on the string of her romper top and smiled when she quickly clasped her hand against her chest. "It's just us here."

His breath was hot against her mouth, and she felt her nipples pebble beneath her hand. "What if someone..." She sucked air through her nose as his mouth closed over her for a brief hard kiss.

"Drop your hand, brat."

Sky hesitated a few seconds before reluctantly lowering her hand. Her body instantly reacted, and her skin prickled with goosebumps as the material fell and the romper slid down her legs.

Quinn kissed his way down her body as he lowered himself to his knees in front of her, taking the waistband of her lacy thong between his teeth and tugging on them until she pushed them over her hips. He longed to bury his tongue between her legs, but he wanted her to come to him this time. He wanted her to want him with a passion so deep she'd be begging him for release. Kissing his way back up her body, he lightly ran his hands down her arms, across her bare stomach and around to cup her ass cheeks. He watched her face as he stepped closer and pressed his hard cock against her stomach. Curving his hands around her ass, he lifted her until her feet left the sand. "Wrap your legs around my waist."

"Quinn, I..." She cried out when she felt him pinch her left ass cheek and her lip protruded in a pout. "What was that for?"

"I think you know. Now, wrap your legs around my waist." When she hesitated, he rested his forehead against her breast bone and kissed the top of her breast. "Trust that I will not do anything other than carry you to the water."

Sky hesitated a few seconds longer before finally wrapping her legs around his waist. Her body instantly reacted to feeling his sun warmed skin pressed against her nakedness and she longed to loosen her legs and sink down on him. Her heart began hammering beneath her ribs when Quinn turned and started for the water, and she began to tremble with her desire. Lowering her head, she kissed the side of his neck, lightly nipping the tan skin with her teeth.

"Unless you want me to fuck you right now, you might want to stop that."

Sky's mouth stilled against his neck, and she slowly lifted her head to look him in the eyes. "And if I did?"

Quinn growled and lifted her higher as he stepped into the water. "Careful what you say brat. Unwrap your legs." When her legs loosened, Quinn pulled her away from his body before releasing his hold on her and letting her drop into the water.

Sky squealed in surprise as she landed in the water and sank beneath the surface. Finding her feet, she pushed herself towards the surface, sputtering and coughing as her head broke free of the water. Wiping her face with one hand, she swatted blindly with the other. "What the fuck did you do that for?" Quinn's voice came from behind her and she spun to face him, her eyes narrowing in annoyance when she saw him smirking at her.

"I figured you needed to cool off a bit."

Sky stepped towards him but he disappeared beneath the water before she could reach him. "Get back here, you coward." Sky shirked when she felt something brush against her calf and she used her arms to propel herself backwards, her eyes frantically scanning the water. "Quinn! Stop playing, this isn't funny anymore."

Quinn slowly stood up behind her and watched her for a few minutes before swimming forward and catching her around the waist. "Calm down, brat. I'm right here."

Sky stilled in his embrace and let him swim them in a slow circle until they were facing away from the beach. "Qui... ummm... Q?" His chest rumbled against her back when he acknowledged her.

"Hmmm?"

"Did you find out who sent Daisy to the cottage?"

Quinn kissed her bare shoulder and up the side of her neck, stopping just below her ear. "It's being handled."

"But who...?"

Catching her chin with his fingertips, he applied slight pressure until she tilted her head to the right. Catching her gaze with is own, he thought about what he wanted to say before speaking. "I don't want you to worry about it, okay? I promise you, it's being handled and it won't happen again."

"So you're not going to tell me who it was?"

Dropping his gaze to her lips, he shook his head before tilting her head back and capturing her mouth in a searing kiss. Easing his hold on her waist, he let his fingers glide over her wet flesh as she turned in his arms, her mouth never leaving his for more than a few seconds. He sucked in a startled breath when she pressed herself against his groin before wrapping her legs around his waist and her arms around his neck. Breaking the kiss, he moved his head back enough to look into her eyes. "Sky?"

A slow smile spread across her face as she tightened her thighs and lifted herself slightly before releasing and rubbing against his hardness as she slide back down.

"You keep that up brat and I'll take you right here in the water."

"And if I want you to?" She lifted again and rolled her hips, rubbing her clit against the hot tip of his cock.

Grabbing her hips, he pulled her away from his body and shook his head. "I won't risk it. When I take you for the first time, I want it to last for hours. Not just a few moments to satisfy a hunger."

Sky opened her mouth to respond but snapped it closed when they heard raised voices coming from the shore. Looking towards the beach, her brow knitted in confusion and she looked back at Quinn, her eyebrow arched in question as she lowered her legs and began treading water.

Quinn dipped his head once in a nod before catching her hand and pulling her after him as he swam toward the shore. Keeping his eyes on the shoreline, he tried to discern where the voices were coming from. When he heard a shout of surprise, his head whipped to the right where a rock wall separated their section of the beach from the neighboring one. Letting his feet sink to the sand below, he walked out of the water and pointed to where Sky had been laying earlier. "Get dressed."

"What about you?" Sky hurried across the sand and snatched up a beach towel, wrapping it around her torso before looking around at Quinn. "You can't mean to go over there naked." Seeing him standing near the rock wall with his hands on his hips, she quickly dried off and pulled on her romper before picking up his towel and jogging over to stand next to him. "Should we intervene?"

Quinn took the towel and wrapped it low on his hips as he continued to listen to the argument from the other side of the wall. "Not just yet."

"But, what if ...?" Her words died away when the woman on the other side spoke again.

"Get away from me! I don't you ever touching me again."

Sky tugged on Quinn's arm and mouthed, 'Daisy' when he looked at her.

Quinn nodded and began walking along the edge of the wall, looking for a way to the other side.

"I gave you a fucking order and you will obey me or suffer the repercussions."

"You don't give me orders anymore, Shadow. You put me in a position with my friend that I never wanted to be in but I did it because I thought Quinn sent the note. Get it through your head, we are finished. Whatever agreement we had is over."

Quinn stepped around the rock wall in time to see Shadow draw his arm back. "If you want to keep that arm, you'll lower it right now."

The man standing over Daisy slowly turned to face Quinn and his top lip lifted in a sneer when he caught sight of Sky standing behind him. "This isn't your business Raven."

Side stepping, Quinn blocked Sky from the man's view and leveled a steely gaze at him. "I'm making it my business, Shadow. Why are you still on the island?"

"I leave when I'm ready, not when you say."

Quinn shifted his gaze to Daisy and inclined his head towards the wall. "Go with Sky."

Daisy had taken three steps when she felt an iron tight grip on her upper arm. Crying out, she looked back at Shadow and tried o pull free of his hold. "Let go of me."

"Don't you dare walk away from me, Little

Flower."

Quinn moved before Sky could stop him and she covered her mouth to hold back a scream when he wrapped his hand around the back of the man's neck. "Let her go, Shadow. Don't make this any harder than it has to be."

Shadow glared down at Daisy before releasing her and holding his hands out to his side. When Quinn shoved him away, he turned to face him, his face red with rage. "I told you to stay out of this. This isn't about you, Raven."

"Isn't it? You sent Daisy to Sky with a note you wrote and signed my name to. You were told to leave the island and yet I find you here attempting to harm Daisy, the very woman you vowed to protect." Quinn crossed his arms over his chest and narrowed his eyes at Shadow. "Why are you still here?"

Instead of answering, the man snapped his fingers at Daisy and pointed to the spot in front of him. "Come here, now."

Sky caught Daisy's arm and began walking backwards, shaking her head at the man she knew as Ben. "She's going with me and you... you can go straight to hell, Benjamin."

Quinn's head jerked back and he turned his gaze on Sky's retreating form, his jaw muscle ticking with suppressed anger. Swallowing down his feelings, he returned his attention to Ben. "I think it's time for you to go, don't you?"

Ben opened his mouth to argue but snapped it closed when he noticed the three men stepping onto the beach. His glare was deadly when he looked back at Quinn. "I hope you enjoy my leftovers."

Every fiber in Quinn's body wanted to lash out in anger but he held himself still as he watched the man Sky had called Benjamin walk over to meet Lance and the two security guards with him.

Lance cast Quinn a quick glance and gave him a brief nod before turning away to follow the other men from the beach.

Quinn released a heavy sigh and looked out across the water. He wanted to ask Sky how she knew Shadow, but he didn't even know if he was entitled to that information. Everyone that came to the resort had a life they kept separate from their time here, and as much as he wanted to push the issue, he resigned to keep his questions to himself. Hell, even he had a life that he never told anyone about. Turning away from the ocean, he made his way back up the beach and around the rock wall.

"How do you know Ben?"

Daisy shrugged and wrapped her arms around her legs as she sat on the couch in Sky's cottage. "I met him at a bar a few weeks ago and thought it'd be fun to bring him here with me. I mean, he seemed very into the lifestyle so I didn't see what it would hurt." Turning her head, Daisy followed Sky with her eyes as she paced around the room chewing the inside of her cheek. "How do you know him?"

Sky stopped pacing and looked at Daisy from the corner of her eye. "I used to … ummm … that is we…"

Daisy's mouth dropped open and she waited for Sky to finish. When she didn't Daisy finished the sentence for her. "The two of you used to fuck? Are you serious? He's not even your type."

"Yeah, I don't usually go for the asshole type." Sky resumed her pacing, her eyes straying to the front door every now and then.

"Are you expecting Q?"

Sky nodded. "He should've been here an hour ago at least. I wonder what's keeping him?"

"Do you want to me to leave? Maybe he knows I'm here and he's giving us privacy?" Daisy stood up and made her way to the door. "I should really go get packed."

Sky stilled and looked at her friend. "You're leaving?"

"I thinks it's best, don't you?"

Sky shook her head. "If you're leaving because of me, don't bother. As soon as I talk to Quinn, I'm outta here."

Daisy's eyes widened. "Wait, why are you leaving?"

"I only planned to stay until tomorrow anyway. Besides, there's nothing for me here, Daisy. I know that now. Don't get me wrong, I love the resort, but I think I'm ready to go home."

"Are you leaving early because of Ben? You know he's been escorted off the island already. Why not just stay until tomorrow?"

Sky remained silent and forced a smile to her lips when there was a knock at the door. "That's probably Quinn at the door now."

"Should I...?" When Sky nodded, Daisy turned the doorknob and pulled the door open. "Yes?"

"Mistress Sky?"

Daisy shook her head and stepped to the side when Sky walked over to stand next her.

"Can I help you?"

The young man standing at the door dipped his head in a nod and waved his hand behind himself. "Master Q sent me to pick you up, Mistress Sky."

Sky met Daisy's quizzical gaze and shrugged before stepping out to follow the young man to the awaiting golf cart.

Chapter 14

Quinn stood on the deck of his cottage and looked out over the ocean. His jaw muscle ticked as he listened to the waves rolling over the sandy beach below and he sighed when his phone beeped behind him. Turning away from the view, he walked over and sat down at the small table before lifting his phone and reading the message there.

TODD:

There's a problem here that requires your attention, bossman.

QUINN:

I'm still on vacation, Todd. Contact Declan to handle it.

TODD:

Can't do that, bossman. Declan
walked off the job two days ago.

QUINN:

TWO DAYS AGO! And you're just
now telling me?

Closing out the text app, Quinn opened the contact list on his phone and quickly selected Declan's number. Pressing the call button, he tapped the speakerphone icon and waited for his brother to answer.

"*What?*"

"You want to tell me why you walked off the job?"

"*Only if you want to tell me why you left that asshole, Blain, in charge.*"

Quinn scowled down at the phone in his hand and resisted the urge to throw it over the railing. "What the hell are you talking about? You know whenever I'm not there you're always in charge."

"*Yeah, well, according to Blain you left him in charge this time and I could either like it or leave, so I fucking left.*"

"Why didn't you call me?"

"*Why would I?*"

"Oh I don't know, Declan. Maybe to ask me if

he was lying. Or to even find out why I would've left him in charge when I never have before. Look, I'll..." Looking over his shoulder towards the front of the cottage, Quinn shook his head when he noticed Sky standing just inside the room beyond. Getting to his feet, he held up a finger to indicate that she should wait before he slid the door closed and turned his back to her. "I'll be heading out soon and I'll be home in a few hours. We can talk about this more when I get there, but I assure you, I absolutely did not leave Blain in charge and I really need you to go to the shop and see what's wrong over there."

"I really don't feel like going to jail today, Quinn."

Sighing, Quinn rubbed his hand over his face and turned back to give Sky a tight lipped smile. "Do this for me... please?"

"Fine, but if I end up in jail, you're bailing me out."

"Deal. Thanks man." Quinn pressed the end icon and slipped his phone into his trouser pocket before pulling the sliding door back open and stepping into the cottage.

Sky took one look at his face and knew she would not be eating the delicious food that was laid out on the table in front of her. "Trouble on the outside?"

Quinn arched an eyebrow and laughed. "You make it sound like we're in prison."

Sky walked over to the table and picked up one of the glasses there before lifting the wine bottle and pouring herself a glass of wine. "I'm leaving tonight."

Quinn watched her empty the glass in one gulp before she refilled her glass and sat the bottle back down. "Any particular reason you're trying to get drunk before you go?"

Sky took a small sip from her glass and shrugged. "Not really. I just..." Sitting the glass down, she reached up and began working the brat pendent through the Q pendent on the necklace. "I guess you'll be wanting this back now. Sorry I wasn't what you were expecting."

Her hand trembled when he placed his fingers over hers, stopping her from removing the necklace. "That's yours to keep. Kind of a momento of your time here."

Lifting her eyes, she met his gaze and bit down on the corner of her bottom lip before nodding once and releasing the two pendents. "If you're sure?"

Quinn squeezed her hand before lifting his own hand and running the pad of his thumb over her bottom lip. "You always nibble your lip when you're nervous, did you know that?"

Sky stayed silent but slowly dipped her head in a brief nod.

"Why are you nervous, Sky?"

"I... you're not mad that I'm leaving when we haven't even...?"

Quinn cocked his head and shook it in response. "Why would I be mad?"

"Because you obviously came to the resort with certain expectations and those were not met."

Quinn cupped the back of her neck and pulled her forward. Lowering his head, he softly kissed her lips before speaking. "You realize I could've gone to anyone else if I was interested in fulfilling those expectations you're so worried about, right?"

Sky's legs grew weak and she reached up to wrap her hands around his wrists. "And... yo... you didn't?" His chuckle vibrated his chest against hers and her nipples grew taught beneath the corset cinched around her body.

"No, brat. I didn't seek out a willing body. I was content to wait for you." Pressing his lips against hers, he deepened the kiss and thrust his tongue inside her mouth when it fell open beneath his.

Sky released his wrists and let her fingers fall to

the buttons on his shirt. Breaking the kiss, she pulled back so she could see what she was doing as she tried unsuccessfully to undo the buttons on his shirt. "Oh for fucks sake." Grasping the material between her hands, she sent the buttons flying as she jerked the shirt open.

Quinn's eyes widened at her aggressiveness but he didn't try to stop her as she pushed the shirt over his shoulders and down his arms. He watched her as she began untying the string holding her dress up and stepped back to gaze at her body as the dress slide to the floor. The corset hugged her body like a second skin and he lifted his hands to run the back of his fingers across the swell of her breasts. "Beautiful." His gaze traveled down her body and stopped at the bare juncture between her thighs. "You shaved?"

"You don't like it?"

Quinn caught Sky's hand when she attempted to cover her nakedness. "I like it very much." Pushing her hand to the side, Quinn covered her lower stomach when his hand and let his fingers rest just above her clit. Lifting his eyes, he waited for her to look at him before he spoke. "I'm going to fuck you before you leave here tonight, you know that, right?"

Sky's mouth twitched as she held back a smile

and she shifted as she spread her legs wider. Her hand settled over his and she pushed at it until he lowered it to cover her heat. "Then stop teasing me and get to it."

Quinn's nostril's flared and his mouth slammed down on top of hers as he curled his fingers into her throbbing core. Pulling his mouth away, he pressed his forehead against hers as he worked his fingers in and out. "You're so hot and wet. I want to taste you."

Stepping away from him, she walked in the direction of the hallway and hoped he would follow her.

Quinn started after her but stopped when his phone began ringing in his pocket. "Son of a bitch." Pulling the phone from his pocket, he thought about ignoring it when he saw Blain's name but knew the man would bug the shit out of him unless he responded. Swiping his finger across the screen, he put the phone to his ear and barked out an unhappy, "What?"

"You can pick Declan up from county lockup when you can be bothered to bring your ass home."

"Can't this wait? I'm a little busy at the moment." Quinn looked up as Sky walked back into the room, the corset now dangling from the tips her fingers.

Sky arched a questioning eyebrow and let the corset fall to the floor before leaning against the door frame and trailing her hand slowly down the length of her naked body, her nipples growing hard as her hand disappeared between her thighs.

Quinn reached down and adjusted his cock and narrowed his eyes at her, shaking his head once before turning his back to her. "Blain, I can't talk right now. Just... don't do anything stupid. I'll be home in a few hours."

"You're leaving?"

Quinn looked over his shoulder at Sky as Blain spoke in his ear.

"If he shows up here ready to fight, I'll ..."

Quinn moved the phone away from his ear and hit the end button before powering it off and laying it on the table. He groaned when Sky picked the corset up from the floor and hurried down the hall toward the bedroom. "Sky, wait." Walking down the hall, he stopped at the bedroom door and watched her attempting to refasten the corset. "Why are you getting dressed?"

"I'm sorry. I should have realized our plans had changed when you didn't come to the cottage." Sky looked around for her dress before remembering she had left it on the floor in the other room.

"I'm not leaving right this minute, Sky." Quinn caught her wrist when she tried to walk around him. His grip was gentle and he looked at the floor when he spoke, his words a soft whisper. "Stay with me, Sky. Just for a little bit?"

Sky slowly looked up at him and knew the game they had been playing with each other was over. This wasn't the domineering man that had spanked her ass the first day he come to her cottage. This was a man that wanted to sleep with her, the real her, and not the brat she had been showing him. Twisting her wrist from his grip, she linked her fingers through his and began walking backwards, pulling him after her as she made her way to the king sized bed sitting in the middle of the room. When the back of her legs touched the bed, she sat down and looked up at him, her eyes holding his for the briefest of moments before she lay back and spread her legs wide. "I believe you said you wanted to taste me."

Quinn's jaw muscles flexed and he drew a deep breath through his nose as he stared down at her, his gaze traveling slowly down her body before returning to her face. "I'm going to make you wish you hadn't waited so long for me to fuck you."

Raising her legs slightly, Sky rested the heels of

her feet on the end of the bed and let her legs fall open as she ran her hands down the inside of her thighs. Her voice was soft and sultry when she spoke. "Are you going to keep standing there talking about it or you going to do it?" Quinn's growl caused her stomach to tighten and she sucked in her breath when he pushed his trousers down his legs before stepping out of them. Her gaze fell to the full hard length of him and she felt herself beginning to throb with anticipation.

Stepping up to the edge of the bed, Quinn placed a hand on each of her thighs and eased them up as he sank to his knees. His nostrils flared as he breathed in the smell of her before lowering his head and swiping his tongue over her heated flesh. Closing his lips over her clit, he hummed and chuckled when Sky's hips bucked beneath his mouth. Releasing her thighs, he circled her core with his middle finger before easing it inside of her. Quinn caressed her lower stomach with his other hand, pressing down when he heard her moans grow louder. Lifting his head, he worked his finger back and forth, curling it upwards as he brought her closer to release.

Sky's fingers clutched at the quilt beneath her and she pressed her ass down into the mattress, her toes curling as her back arched. "Q! Don't... stop."

Giving her clit one final lick, Quinn pulled his hand away and got to his feet. He smiled down at Sky when her eyes flew open in shock. "You don't come until I tell you to, remember?"

"But I thought..."Her words died away and she squeaked in surprised when Quinn used her legs to flip her over onto her stomach. "Oh!"

Grasping her hips, Quinn lifted her up on to her knees and caressed the globes of her ass before pulling her back to him and resting the tip of his cock against her wet heat. "Tell me you want me to fuck you."

"Wha... what?" Looking back over her shoulder, Sky saw his neck muscles straining from him holding himself back from entering her.

Quinn's words come out rough when he spoke though clenched teeth. "Tell... me you want me to fuck you."

In answer, Sky pressed back against him and shuddered as the tip of his cock slipped inside. "Fuck me, Quinn."

Throwing his head back, Quinn slammed into her fully and tightened his hold on her hips when she tried to pull away. "You're pussy is so hot and tight." Leaning forward, he bit the back of her neck and rolled his hips before pulling out and slamming forward again. Grasping a fistful of her hair, he pulled her head back and caught her lips as he moved within her in slow powerful thrusts. Ending the kiss, he pressed his mouth to her ear. "What do you want, Sky?"

Sky shook her head and tired to pull her hair free, crying out when he tightened his hold.

"Tell me what you want." He bit down on his bottom lip when Sky's hand slapped down on his thigh and she pulled forward, urging his to move faster. "Say it, Sky. Tell me what you desire."

"Faster... I want you to fuck me faster and harder."

Releasing her hair, he sat back up and grasped her hips again, his teeth sinking into his bottom lip as he stared down at them joined together, his cock slick with her essence as he began rocking his hips faster. He was transfixed by the way her pussy was sucking his cock and he pumped harder and faster, driving them both towards release.

"Quinn!"Hearing his name from her mouth, he slapped her ass and groaned when her muscles clamped down on him, pulling him deeper as she fought to keep from coming. Smacking her again, he gave her the command that she had been needing g to hear. "Come for me, Sky."

Sky's body stiffened and her cries grew louder as her orgasm washed through her. Her nipples tingled where they rubbed against the bed as she rocked with Quinn's thrusts. Her body shuddered and her arms grew weak. Lowering her head to the bed, she sucked in a breath when she felt Quinn's hot cum land on her back. Raising her head, she looked back at him and smiled. "You know you're going to have to wash that off in the shower, right?"

Giving her ass a light smack, Quinn winked at her as he rubbed away the pain. "I was planning on it." Turning away, he spoke as he walked towards the bathroom. "Don't move. I'll be right back with a washcloth."

Sky sighed and slowly lowered her body to the bed. Folding her arms beneath her head, she watched the bathroom door, a sated smile curving her lips, and waited for Quinn to return. The delish tingle between her legs caused her to smother a laugh as Quinn walked back into the room.

"Care to share the joke?"

Sky held still while he cleaned her back off. "It's nothing really."

Quinn scoffed and swatted her naked ass. "Liar. Tell me what's so funny."

Rolling onto her side, she curled one leg up and raised herself up onto her elbow. "You were right, ya know."

"Oh baby, I usually am." Quinn winked at her and laughed softly when she pushed herself into a sitting position and reached for his pillow. He ducked when she threw it at his head, his laughter growing louder when he lunged towards the bed, catching her by the wrists and pinning her beneath him. His mouth captured hers in a deep kiss and he shifted until his cock rested between her thighs.

Sky arched her hips upward until she felt him pressed against her core. Her breath caught in her throat as she moved her hips, rubbing herself along the hardened length of him. Each time the tip of his arousal touched her clit, she released a tiny breathy moan.

Quinn closed his eyes and matched her rhythm. "Keep it up brat and I'll fuck you raw before this night is over."

Threading her fingers through his hair, Sky pulled his head down until his ear was next to her mouth. "Is that supposed to be a threat?"

Quinn's eyes flew open and he leaned back so he

could watch her face as he invaded her body in one swift thrust. "That's a fucking promise, brat."

A feminine growl rumbled up from her chest and she wrapped her arms tightly around his shoulders before pushing him over onto his back. Straddling him, Sky leaned down, her hair cascading around them, and guided him back to her entrance. Her mouth found his as she lowered herself onto him, her hips rolling in a slow circle.

Quinn gripped her hips and tried to hold her still. Breaking the kiss, he sucked air between his teeth and pressed his head into his pillow. "What are you doing to me, woman? You're going to make me come quick if you keep moving like that." His fingers bit into her flesh and he released a groan of pleasure as she continued to ride him.

Throwing her head back, Sky chuckled and lifted her arms to the back of her neck, arching her back and pushing her breasts high. "You don't come until I tell you that you can." Her laughter filled the room when he released one of her hips and delivered a stinging swat to her ass.

"Cheeky, wench."

Falling forward, Sky caught herself with her hands and looked down at him briefly before capturing his mouth with hers once more.

Chapter 15

"So, you ready to tell me how it went? I'm guessing your mini vacation was a success."

Sky smiled at her sister's reflection in the mirror and continued brushing her hair. "It was... memorable." Setting her brush down, she turned and leaned back against her vanity, cocking her head to the side as she studied her sister's flushed cheeks. "Dare I ask what you've been up to while I was away?"

Sunni straightened from her relaxed position and turned away from the room, her hair flying out behind her. "Nothing. What's for supper?"

Sky's eyes widened and she hurried from the room after her sister. "Something happened ? What? You finally met someone, didn't you? Who is he?"

Shrugging nonchalantly, Sunni pretended to read through the menu's they kept by the computer. "You wouldn't know them. How does Dom's sound? We can get lasagna or cheesy spaghetti with five cheese garlic toast."

Sky's cheeks heated and she turned her head away. "That's... uhh... that's fine."

Sunni arched an eyebrow and stared at her sister as she noticed the color staining her neck. "What happened on your vacation, Skyler?"

Sky looked back at Sunni and debated telling the truth. Deciding against it, she changed the subject. "Did anyone call while I was gone?"

"Ben called, multiple times before I left."

"What did he want?" Sky picked up the stack of mail on her desk and began shuffling through it.

"I don't know, I never answered. I thought you two were over?" When Sky nodded without answering, Sunni began dialing the number to Dom's.

Sky waited for Sunni to finish placing their order before holding up a manila envelope and speaking. "Why didn't you telling about this?"

Sunni remained silent as she walked across the room and took the envelope from her sister. Her eyes widened and she handed it back. "You open it. If it's a rejection, don't tell me."

Picking up the letter opener, Sky slit the top of the envelope open and pulled the documents from inside. She silently read the top letter before looking at Sunni and sighing. "Well damn."

"I knew it. They rejected my application. I don't know what I was thinking when I applied to…"

"You're in."

"…that culinary school. They never… wait. What?"

Tears filled Sky's eyes and she nodded when Sunni looked at her. "You're in! Oh, Sunni! You're going to be living in Paris!" Sky caught her sister when she launched herself into her arms and hugged her, squinting and moving her head away as Sunni's squeals of excitement filled the room.

Pulling away, Sunni wiped the tears from beneath her eyes and finally took the documents from Sky. "Do you mind going to Dom's to pick up supper? I want to read through this and call…"

Sky waited for her to finish her sentence and shook her head when she walked away instead. "Sure thing. I'll be back in a bit." Picking up her keys, she walked from the house and slid behind the steering wheel of her car.

"This can't be fucking happening again." Pulling to the side of the road, Sky turned the engine off before pushing her door open looking towards the back tire. She was stepping from the car when she remembered that she never took her tire in to be repaired. "Great. Just fucking fantastic." Sitting back in the driver's seat, she looked towards her handbag where she had the card Quinn had left when he changed her tire. Her stomach tensed as she reached for her bag and pulled the card out, her gaze landing on his name. "Quinn." His name whispered past her lips as a sigh and she picked up her phone and began dialing the number he had written down. Pressing the phone to her ear, she leaned her head back against the headrest and closed her eyes as she waited for him to answer.

Quinn growled in frustration and swiped the screen of his phone. "What?"

"Uhhh, is this... Sorry, I'm looking for Quinn. Is he available?"

Quinn instantly recognized the voice on the other end of the phone and his body stilled. Staring up at the open crank case above him, he cleared his throat and responded. "Sky?"

"Qu... Quinn?"

"Yeah. What's up?" He heard her release a long drawn out breath and he pushed the creeper he was laying on from beneath the truck. Sitting up, he waved Declan over and motioned towards the truck as he stood. "Is something wrong?"

"Well, remember the card you left telling me to get my tire fixed?"

"You called me to schedule an appointment for your tire repair?"

"Ummm, not exactly. Anyway you can send someone out to Vista Valley with a spare?"

Quinn dropped his head and pinched the bridge of his nose, his mouth twitching as he forced himself not to laugh out loud. "Of course. You just sit tight and they'll be there shortly." Pressing the red end icon, Quinn huffed out a chuckle and looked down at his grease stained jeans. "Declan, I have to go out on a service call. Keep an eye on the place, will ya?"

"Sure thing, Quinn."

Pocketing his phone, Quinn walked out of the shop and climbed up into his truck, his heart kicking up with excitement at seeing Sky again.

Sky jumped and placed a hand over her heart as she turned to look out her car window. Her eyes noted the grease stained jeans and dirty hands of the man that had knocked on the glass and her sigh of disappointment filled the air as she turned her car to the axillary position and lowered her window. "Did Quinn tell you that my spare is also flat?" Turning her head, her eyes collided with his and her heart skipped a beat. "Quinn." His name was a breathy whisper and her lips curled into a smile of happiness and longing.

Quinn's eyes dropped to the necklace dangling between her breasts before he returned her smile. "Brat."

They stared at each other for a few minutes

before Quinn motioned towards her rear tire. "I'm beginning to think you might have an enemy."

Sky rolled her eyes and shook her head. "There's construction near my house and I think I'm picking up nails or something." Reaching for the door handle, she waited for Quinn to step back before pushing the door open and stepping out of the car to stand beside him. "So... how have you been?"

Quinn's smile broadened and he looked down at her, his gaze traveling over her body. "It's only been two days since I last saw you and I can't stop thinking about you, if that tells you anything."

Heat flooded her lower stomach and her body tingled as she remembered their last night together. "It feels like it's been a lot longer." She swayed towards him, her eyes drifting closed in anticipation of his lips on hers.

Quinn cleared his throat and caught her by the shoulders before stepping back. "I need to get your tire fixed so I can get back to the shop."

Sky's cheeks flushed with embarrassment and she looked down at her feet and nodded. "Right... umm... well, I don't, uhh, I don't have a spare tire."

Quinn scratched the back of his neck and looked over his shoulder towards his truck. "It's fine. I brought one you can use until you can get both of yours fixed." Without waiting for a reply, Quinn turned and walked to the back of his truck.

Sky lifted her head enough to look at him as she silently berated herself for being foolish enough to think he would still be interested in her. His words played through her head, *'I can't stop thinking about you'* and she felt her embarrassment turning to anger at herself. She knew their time together was nothing serious and yet she had built it up in her mind to be more than it was. She knew, if she had sex with him, she'd probably develop feelings for him, but she did it anyway. And now, here she stood, looking like an idiot because she tried to kiss the man when all he was doing was his job.

Quinn walked back to the car carrying a spare and jack. "When I get this changed, I'll take both of your tires back with me and get them repaired or replaced, whichever you want."

Sky walked around the back of the car to stand on the shoulder of the road while he changed the tire. "I'd rather have them replaced. I know I'd be in a constant state of worry if I got them plugged."

Quinn broke the lug nuts loose before jacking the car up and nodded his understanding. "I may have to order them and they'll run you about a hundred dollars or more each."

Sky watched a car speed by them and folded her arms over her chest as she spoke. "Cost isn't an issue."

Quinn didn't miss the way she pursed her lips before she answered him and he shook his head as he returned his attention to changing the tire. "I never meant to insinuate that it was."

Sky looked everywhere but at him as a breeze kicked up and sent his masculine scent towards her. "How long do you think it'd be before you can get them?"

"A few days, a week at most." Standing, Quinn lowered the car back to the ground before picking up the flat tire and his jack. "Let me get these in the truck and I'll come back for the other one."

Sky hated the small talk. She wanted to throw herself into his arms, grease be damned. She wanted him to hold her, kiss her, touch her. Hell, anything would be better than this bullshit. Kicking the gravel at her feet, she walked back around the car and leaned in the open window to push the button for the trunk. Her body stiffened when she felt his hands encircle her waist and the heat from his body as he leaned against her back.

"Have dinner with me Friday?"

Sky didn't even need to think about her answer.

She instantly nodded in agreement and sighed when he pushed her hair to the side and kissed the back of her neck before releasing her and stepping to the back of the car. Turning, she watched him lift the tire from the trunk before slamming it closed and walking back towards her. "Do you...? I should give you my address."

Quinn nodded and waited for her as she leaned back into the car. His gaze fell to the curve of her ass and his hands ached to touch her. When she leaned back out of the car, he pretended to be focused on her tire. "You sure you don't want this back for a spare?"

Sky chuckled as she wrote her address on the napkin she had found in her console. "I think we can stop this 'not interested' small talk, don't you?" Turning, she held the napkin out towards him and cocked her head to the side as she waited for him to take it. "You should know that I have a very nosey sister that lives with me. She's going to want to grill you like she's working with law enforcement when you come to pick me up. Don't feel obligated to tell her anything you don't feel comfortable sharing."

Taking the napkin, Quinn looked at the address and his brows shot up. Looking up at her, he held the napkin back out to her.

Sky's face fell and she looked from his face to the napkin and back again, her expression one of hurt confusion. "I don't understand."

"I know where this is."

Her brow furrowed and she took the napkin back. "Umm, how exactly do you know where I live?"

"My brother lives a few houses down the road. I've always wondered who lived in the big house down that path."

"That'd be us. We inherited the place from our grandmother a few years ago. If you want, you can come over tonight for supper and I'll show you around the place. I was actually on my way to pick up our order and there's more than enough for three." Sky couldn't believe her own forwardness, but she refused to rescind the invitation.

"Are you sure? I'd love to get a look at the place."

Sky smiled and nodded. "Absolutely. What time should I expect you?"

Quinn looked at his watch before settling on a time with her. He stepped back and watched as she climbed back into her car and waited for her to drive away.

Turning the key in the ignition, Sky started the

car before poking her head back out the window. "What do I owe you?"

Quinn lifted his hand and waved her question away. "You're fine with this service call. I'll bring you a quote for the tires when I come over later."

Sky studied him for a few more seconds before pulling her head back into the car and shifting into drive. Giving him a wave, she pulled out into the street and drove away, her eyes going to the rearview mirror every few seconds until she could no longer see Quinn.

Chapter 16

Sky watched the clock over the fireplace mantle as she set the table and got the food from the oven. "Sunni, can you look outside and make sure the driveway lights are on? I don't want him missing it."

Sunni rolled her eyes and sat her book down as she stood to do as her sister asked. Pulling the curtain back, she looked outside. "I think he's here."

Sky was suddenly a bundle of nervous energy as she hurried around the living room , straightening throw pillows that didn't need straightening and folding the lap quilt that Sunni had been using. "Please be nice to him, Sunni. I really like him and..." Her words faded when she heard two doors slam outside. "He brought someone?"

Sunni remained silent and nodded as she walked

over to the front door and turned the deadbolt before pulling the door open. Her mouth dropped as she stared at the two men walking up the sidewalk. Closing her mouth, she plastered a welcoming smile across her face and held the door open wider when they stepped up onto the porch. "Welcome. Won't you come in?" Sunni closed the door behind them and looked at Sky, her eyes wide as she mouthed, "Oh my goodness."

Sky looked from Quinn to the man standing at his side and waited for Quinn to make the introductions.

"Sky, Sunni, I'd like you to meet my brother." Quinn pointed at each woman as he made the introductions. "Declan, this is Sky and her sister Sunni."

Declan tore his gaze away from Sunni and held his hand out towards Sky. "Pleasure to finally meet you. Quinn has tolll..." His words ended on a grunt when Quinn elbowed him in the ribs. "What the shit, man?"

Quinn ignored his brother and held his hand out toward Sunni. "Nice to meet you. I'm Quinn, the guy who fixed your sister's flat... twice."

Sky released a relieved sigh upon hearing Quinn's introduction and smiled as she waved toward the dining room. "If you two would like to eat now, I'll set another place for Declan while you wash up."

"Sorry I didn't call to make sure it was okay to bring a guest. I guess I wasn't thinking."

Sky motioned for them to follow her as she made her way into the kitchen. "It's okay. I ordered a little extra when I finally got to the restaurant this afternoon." Looking over her shoulder, she slightly nodded her head and motioned with her eyes for Sunni to join them in the kitchen before she continued speaking. "Did you have to order the tires?"

Quinn shook his head and reached for a hand towel. "I had a set of new ones that size at the shop. Not sure how you feel about your tires matching though."

"They don't match?"

Quinn looked over at Sunni and shook his head again. "They don't match what's currently on the car, no. But your sister can always come to the shop and I can switch out the rest to match. She can use one of the other tires that's already on the car as a spare." Quinn passed the hand towel to Declan and turned to face Sky as he waited for her to answer.

Carrying the extra place setting into the dining room, Sky set the plate down in front of the empty chair opposite Sunni's and began arranging the silverware. "I'll have to remember to call next week and set up a time to bring the car in."

"Or you can just bring it in this weekend."

Sky stood up straight and turned to find Quinn standing directly behind her. Her throat bobbed when she swallowed and the tip of her tongue darted out of her mouth as she licked her lips. "You don't mind?"

Catching her chin between his thumb and forefinger, Quinn ran the pad of his thumb over her bottom lip and stepped in closer. Lowering his head, he caught her lips with his and nibble lightly until her mouth dropped open.

Sky whimpered with longing and wrapped her arms around his neck to pull him closer as she deepened the kiss. The room they were in faded from thought, her sister and his brother forgotten as she wrapped her fingers into his hair, holding him still as she pressed herself against his body, his muscles feeling like steel against her breasts. The kissed ended all too soon and her face flushed red as she caught the open mouthed look on her sisters face. Dropping her arms, she waited for Quinn to move before she tugged at the bottom of her shirt and looked at the floor. "Drinks?"

Quinn's face was lit with amusement as he watched Sky hurry into the kitchen, catching her sister's arm and pulling her after her on her way by. Looking at his brother, he waved at the chair in front of him before walking to the end of the table.

Sitting, Declan propped his arms on the table and leaned towards his brother. Keeping his voice low, he spoke to Quinn in a horse whisper of disapproval. "That was a hell of a hello, Quinn. I was getting ready to take Sunni outside so y'all could fuck right here on the table."

Quinn met his brother's eyes and arched an eyebrow. "And what were your plans for Sunni?"

Declan sat up in his chair and spread a napkin in his lap, avoiding further eye contact with Quinn. "How long have you two known each other?"

"Not long, but long enough."

"So you two are a couple?" Declan chanced a look at Sunni and wondered if she might be single. His gaze dropped to the curve of her ass when she bent over and he bit down on his bottom lip.

"Careful there, little brother. I'm not sure how Sky will feel about you ogling her kid sister like that." Quinn smiled as Sky walked back into the room carrying two glasses and a bottle of wine.

"She's hardly a kid and... she can take care of

herself." Extending the wine bottle towards him, she waited for him to take it before reaching into her back pocket and getting the corkscrew she had put there while in the kitchen and handing that to him as well before sitting a glass in front of him and walking back to her place at the table.

Sunni came into the dining room carrying two more glasses and sat one in front of Declan before leaning down near his ear and dropping her voice to a whisper. "You free this Friday night?" When he nodded, she chuckled and spoke again. "You want to go to a concert with me then?"

Leaning to the side, Declan stared at her full lips before lifting his gaze to hers. "I'd rather take you out for pizza and a movie."

Sunni's smile fell and she stood to walk around the table. Once seated, she passed her glass to Quinn to fill before speaking. "I've had these tickets for months and I really do want to see this band. Perhaps we can work something out at a later time?"

Declan saw his opportunity with Sunni dwindling away and quickly shook his head. "I mean, I'd love a pizza and movie night, but I'm not against going to a concert. What's the band?"

Sunni told Declan the name of the band and they began making plans for the following Friday.

Sky focused her attention on her plate and remained silent throughout the rest of the meal. Once everyone had finished, she helped Sunni clear the table and wash the dishes while the two men discussed the day they had at work earlier.

"He's cute."

Sky looked over at Sunni and nodded. "They both are."

"You don't mind if I go out with Declan this Friday then?"

Sky stopped washing the plate and rested her hands in the sink of hot soapy water as she studied her sister's worried face. "Why would I mind? You're going out with Declan is perfectly okay with me. I'm only interested in his brother."

Sunni put her elbows on the counter and rested her chin in her hands as she studied the two men still sitting at the dining room table. "I don't know. I just don't want it to get weird. We've never dated brothers before."

Continuing washing the dishes, Sky chuckled and held the plate out for Sunni to rinse. "It will only be weird if you make it weird. Now, let's hurry up so we can get back in there before they decide to leave."

Nodding in agreement, Sunni took the plate from Sky and turned the water on.

"Do you plan to get horses?"

Sky shook her head and looked around the barn. "I don't have any plans for that right now. I stay too busy to keep them worked properly and I don't want to get an animal just to neglect it."

Quinn walked over to a wooden ladder that led up to the loft and rested his foot on the bottom rung. "I can understand that. I also respect you for putting an animals best interest ahead of any desire you may have to own one. Not many people do that."

"I'm not like other people."

"I'm beginning to see that." Turning, Quinn began to climb up the ladder. Reaching the top, he climbed into the hay loft and turned to look down at Sky. "Care to join me up here?"

Sky smirked up at him and cocked her head to the side. "Any reason you trying to get me in a dark secluded place, Q?" Lifting her hand, she toyed with the necklace she hadn't wanted to take off when she returned home.

In answer, Quinn grasped he bottom of his shirt

and pulled it over his head before dropping it at his feet. "No reason at all, brat." His hands dropped to his belt and he began to unbuckle it as Sky grasped the lower rung of the ladder.

Sky fought down her fear of heights as she climbed up the ladder. Reaching the top, she stared up at Quinn and sucked in a breath when his hardened cock sprang out to greet her. Climbing into the loft, she crawled as far away from the edge as she could before standing and turning to face him. Her legs trembled with a mixture of fright and longing. "I... I can't be that close to the edge."

Without saying a word, Quinn walked over to her before pushing his jeans down his legs and stepping free of them. Catching her face between his palms, he lowered his head and captured her mouth in a brief, deep kiss. Lifting his head, rubbed her cheeks with his thumbs before letting his hands travel down her neck to her breasts.

Sky arched into his hands and sucked a hissing breath through her teeth when he gently pinched her nipples through her shirt and bra. With trembling fingers, she began to unbutton her shirt, stopping short when he placed his hands over hers.

"Let me do it." When she lowered her hands, Quinn finished unbuttoning her shirt and pushed it over her arms before letting it drift to the floor as he reached for the front snap of her bra. When her breasts spilled free of the material, he took one of her nipples between his lips and sucked it greedy as he worked her loose skirt up over her hips.

Sky whimpered with longing as she felt his hands caressing her inner thighs and she parted her legs to allow him access to her throbbing flesh. She held her breath, slightly begging him to move her thong to the side and she cried out with joy when he answered her unspoken need. She arched into his fingers and her nails bit into his forearms as she rode the waves of pleasure his fingers were bringing her. When he pushed her skirt down her hips, she stepped out of it and waited for him to spread it on the floor, her pussy throbbing with need and longing for his fingers again. She allowed him to lower her to the floor of the loft and she spread her legs wider as he kissed his way down her stomach. She wanted to stop him, to tell him she felt dirty, but hearing his growl of desire as he breathed in her scent, she threaded her fingers through his hair and urged him to go lower.

Quinn lifted her up and held her as he buried his face between her creamy thighs and thrust his tongue against the petal-soft folds of her womanhood. Her cries of ecstasy filled the loft as she rode his mouth and he grasped her hips to hold her still as his tongue darted back and forth.

"Please, please. I need... I want you to..."

Giving her clit one final swipe with his tongue, Quinn lifted his head and met her gaze as he circled her clit with his thumb. His cock twitched as he pressed it against her opening and he hesitated briefly before burying himself balls deep inside her warmth with a single thrust of his hips.

Sky threw her hands over her head and ground herself against Quinn's groin, a smile a satisfaction curving her mouth up. "Yes. Fuck me harder."

Quinn's jaw flexed as he gripped her hips tighter and pulled almost all the way out before driving forward again, this time hard enough to make Sky cry out in pain. He stopped and stared down at her, horrified that he had hurt her. As he was opening his mouth to apologize, she shimmed her hips and spoke in a whisper.

"Again."

He held back a cry of his own as he slammed into her again, each thrust as hard as the last. He felt her tighten around his cock and knew she was on the cusp of release. His neck muscles strained as he held back his own climax as she clinched tighter around him, his cock growing slick with her desire.

Sky opened her eyes and stared up at Quinn as she continued to rock her hips to met his thrusts. She wanted to watch him as he came. She wanted to see what her body could do to him. When she felt him swelling within her, she tightened her legs to hold him inside.

Quinn gritted his teeth and held himself back from coming as he stared down into her face. He wanted to spill inside her, to feel her pulsating heat surrounding him as he came. He held her gaze with questioning eyes and, when she gave a small nod, he cried out and thrust inside her a final time, his head fallen back as his own orgasm rocked his body.

Quinn held Sky's hand as he helped her off the last rung of the ladder. When she turned to face him, he leaned down and kissed her swiftly before linking his fingers with hers and walking towards the barn door. Stepping out into the night, he pulled up short and cocked his head as if listening for something.

Sky opened her mouth to ask him what he was listening for when a feminine moan of pleasure filled the night air. "Oh, ummm, maybe we should wait a bit before going back inside the house?"

Quinn chuckled as he nodded in agreement. "I think maybe we should." Tugging her against his side, he wrapped an arm around her shoulders and turned to walk in the opposite direction. "I thought I saw an outbuilding back here when I pulled into the yard tonight."

Sky nodded and tightened her arms around his waist. "There's a guest house back here. It's not set up to be lived in though."

"It's unlivable then?"

"Oh, it's livable. We just never saw a need to set it up. Sunni and I agreed that we'd share the big house until one of us decided we'd be more comfortable living out here. So far, we prefer living in the same house." When they stepped up onto the guest house porch, Sky released Quinn and walked over to an old rocking chair sitting near a window.

Quinn stared in amazement when she turned the rocker onto its side and pulled a key from somewhere beneath it. "You're not worried someone will find that key?"

Sky shook her head as she turned to unlock the

door. "They'd have to know where to look and even if they thought to look there, they'd still not find it." When they stepped inside, Sky flipped on a light before turning to show the key to Quinn.

Quinn stared down at the piece of burlap in her palm before reaching into her hand and turning it over. The key to the guest house was glued to the burlap and was undetectable when flipped over to the other side. "That's the craziest shit I've seen in a while. Fantastic and clever, but still crazy."

Sky wrapped her fingers around the key as she nodded and reached around him to close the door. "I'd offer you something to drink but..." With a wave of her hand, she brought his attention to the sparingly furnished rooms beyond. "It's just about completely empty in here. If you'll excuse me, I'll be right back."

Quinn watched her disappear down a narrow hallway before turning his attention to the spacious room in front of him. A couch sat facing the fireplace and Quinn walked over and sat down, his leg bouncing nervously as he waited for Sky to come back.

"Sorry about that."

Quinn turned and smiled when Sky reached back and plucked hay from her hair. Standing, he walked over to her and kiss the tip of her nose as he reached around her and cupped her ass. "This place would make a perfect weekend retreat."

Sky tilted her head to give him access to her neck. "I don't want strangers here."

Quinn nipped the skin just below her ear and caressed her pert nipples with his thumbs. "I meant for us."

Sky's eyes had been drifting closed but they flew open as the meaning of his words sank in. Pushing back enough to see his face, she studied his expression for a few seconds before responding. "Are you serious? You want to keep seeing me?"

Pulling her close again, he rested his forehead against hers and nodded. "I'm completely serious. Do you oppose the idea?" Quinn held his breath as he waited for her to answer. Relief flooded through him when she slowly shook her head. Catching her face between his hands, he nibbled at her bottom lip before raining gentle kisses across her face. Returning to her mouth, he caught her bottom lip between his teeth and tugged until her mouth fell open, offering him the entrance that he sought.

Sky's legs threatened to buckle as his tongue delved into her mouth. His kiss was hard but gentle and she felt her lower stomach flutter with need once again. Pulling back, her breathing rapid, she covered her mouth with a trembling hand and turned away from him. "I need..."

His breath was ragged and deep when he spoke. "What? What do you need?"

Sky ran her fingers through her hair and turned to face him, a bewildered smile on her face. "I don't know." Looking around the room, she could envision what she'd do to it to make it into a place for just the two of them. The idea that they could actually be a couple or more scared the shit out of her. Looking back at him, she swallowed several times and took a deep calming breath through her nose. "I need to think about it."

"Think about what?"

"You... me... us. Quinn, I know me and I don't know how long I can be in a casual relationship with someone like you."

Quinn's brow furrowed and he crossed his arms over his massive chest as he stood to his full height and looked down at her. "Someone like me? What exactly do you mean someone like me?"

Sky released a humorless laugh and waved at him. "Look at you. You exude sex. When you're near me all I can think about is jumping your bones. I know eventually sex won't be enough for me. I'll want all of you. Your body and your heart. I'll fall for you and I don't know that I'd be able to pick myself back up when you discard me like a used tissue."

Quinn stared at her dumbfounded. Sky was the last person he expected to hear those words from and he was unsure how to respond. His mouth opened and closed as he tried to form a sentence but, when she turned and walked to the front door, he closed his mouth and followed after her. "Sky?"

Stepping from the guesthouse, she waited for him to join her on the porch before pulling the door closed and twisting the key in the lock. Keeping her back to him, she walked to the rocker and knelt to replace the key. "I think we both need time to figure out where we want to go from here." Standing, she finally faced him and reached up to brush her hair back from her face as the wind picked up around them. "I could love you, Quinn and I don't know how that makes me feel right now." Looking away from him, she made her way down the steps and across the lawn towards the house.

Quinn stood on the porch, his hands in his pockets, and watched her walk away from him as her words echoed through his mind. '*I could love you.*'

Chapter 17

Sky stood beside Sunni and swiped at the tears coursing down her face. "I hate this. I'm so happy for you but I still hate it."

Sunni swallowed back her own tears and nodded as she wrapped Sky up in a hug. "I promise to call as often as I can."

Sky returned the hug and forced herself to let go when Sunni stepped back. "You better."

"What are you going to do without me?"

Sky released a watery laugh and sniffed. "Me? I think I should be asking what you're going to do without me."

"Miss, we need you to board now."

Sunni nodded at the young woman standing by the jetway and gave Sky's hands a slight squeeze, her face filled with sad excitement. "I love you, sis and I'll call when I get to my hotel."

With one final hug, the two sisters parted ways and Sky waved until she could no longer see Sunni. She let her tears flow freely as she watched the plane depart, her heart already feeling the distance between them.

Sky was pacing the living room, sipping from a glass of wine when the house phone rang. Rushing across the room, she jerked the receiver up and put it against her ear, speaking sharply before the caller could. "What the fuck do you mean waiting this long to call?"

"What's wrong with your cell?"

Sky looked towards the couch where her cellphone lay and shook her head. "Nothing. Now answer the question. Do you know how worried I've been about you? I thought something happened and no one knew to contact me."

"Sky, I've been trying to call you. Your phone rings a few times and goes straight to voicemail. I just wanted

you to know that made it safely and the room is fantastic. I'm going to be busy for the next few days but I'll call you every night. I have to go, Sky. I love you"

"Sunni, I..." Sky sighed and pulled the phone away from her ear when she heard three beeps. Replacing the receiver, she turned and scowled at her cellphone before walking over and picking it up. Pressing the side button, she waited for the screen to light up and released a string of heated words when the screen remained black. "Guess it's time for a new one anyway." Putting the phone in her back pocket, she picked her keys up from the side table and headed for the front door.

Sky picked up her glass of tea and took a sip, her attention focused on the couple across the street. "I told him I could love him."

Daisy coughed and quickly covered her mouth with her napkin.

Concern filled Sky's eyes and she stood and hurried around the table to pat her friend on the back, certain she was choking on her spaghetti.

When Daisy took a deep breath and picked up the glass of water sitting in front of her, Sky returned to her place at the table and leaned towards forward. "Are you okay?"

Daisy nodded as she drank. Sitting the glass down, she wiped her eyes and cleared her throat. Her voice was raspy when she finally spoke. "Did I hear you right? You told Quinn, aka the Raven, that you could love him?"

"The Raven?"

"Yeah, and I'm guessing he got that name because of those black ass wings tattooed across his back." When she noticed Sky's attention shift, she snapped her fingers in the other woman's face until she looked back at her. "Spill it. Why would you tell him that?"

Sky sipped from her glass again and sat back, shrugging nonchalantly. "Because it's true. I thought my time at the resort would be fun and a break from the monotony of my everyday life. Instead I found a man that made me feel more alive than anyone else ever has. I found a man that I can see myself growing old with and still loving him when he's old, fat, and bald. I found someone that I don't think I could let go if things didn't work out."

Daisy studied her through narrowed eyes before

picking up her own glass of tea and lifting it to her lips. "And you told him all of this?"

Sky avoided eye contact and shook her head. "I told him a variation of what I just told you, and... and then I walked away."

"You walked away?"

Sky nodded and chewed the inside of her cheek. "I haven't seen or spoken to him since."

Daisy released a low whistle. "I can't believe you walked away from him. When did this all happen?"

Sky looked up from beneath her lashes. "The end of summer... last year."

"*Six months ago!* Are you...? You can't be serious? He could've moved on by now. Did you ever think of that?"

Sky sat her glass down and cocked her head at Daisy. "Of course I've thought about it. Every time I've picked up the phone to call him, I've thought about it. Every time I look at his business card stuck to my fridge, I wonder if he's seeing someone and forgotten all about me. He never called me after that night, you know. Maybe I scared him off?"

"Here's a thought. Call him! Hell go one step further and send him nudes." Daisy laughed as a look of mortification settled over Sky's face.

"And if he's in a relationship?"

Daisy reached across the table and laid her hand on top of Sky's, a soft smile curving her lips upwards. "Honey, call the man."

Sky returned Daisy's smile and hesitated before nodding. "I'll think about it, promise." As Daisy sat back and picked up her glass again, Sky looked down at her brand new phone and wondered if she'd ever be able to make the call.

Chapter 18

Sky's heart thundered against her ribs and she smoothed her hands over the front of the leather corset before touching the steel cuffs encircling her wrists. Stepping over to the dresser, she picked up the bluetooth remote and a single rose. Holding the flower and remote in the same hand, she took a deep breath before striking a sexy pose and pressing down on the shutter button of the remote. Hurrying over to the camera, she looked at the photo and smirked as she sent it to her phone before taking up position in front of the camera again and plucking a petal from the rose, letting it fall as she bent over in front of the camera and pressed the shutter button again.

Quinn grunted as he bared down on the ratchet, ignoring his phone when it dinged for the third time. His frustration mounted when it dinged for a fourth time and he raised his voice to be heard over the radio. "Declan, will you see who the fuck is blowing up my phone?" A low whistle came from behind him and he raised up enough to see his brother holding his phone, his eyes wide as he tried to shield it from Todd's prying eyes. "What are the two of you looking at?" When they didn't answer, he laid the ratchet on the engine block and wiped his hands as he walked across the garage. Snatching the phone from his brother's hand, he glared at Declan until he walked away before turning the phone over and looking at the screen. His cock instantly hardened behind his grease stained jeans and desire coursed through his veins. Looking at Sky posed so provocatively with steel wrapped around her wrists and rose petals at her feet made him remember the feel of her body shuddering beneath his as he brought her to the edge. Clearing his throat, he turned to tell Declan that he was leaving but, seeing his brother holding the ratchet, he knew he didn't have to say anything. Looking at the photo once more, he stomped from the garage and straddled his motorcycle, groaning at the vibration between his legs when he brought the motor to life.

Sky looked up from her laptop and cocked her head as she listened to the sound of a deep rumble. Getting up, she walked over to the front door and moved the curtain to the side. Her breath left her in a rush when she saw the motorcycle speeding up the long drive. "Quinn." His name fell from her lips as a breathy whisper as she reached to turn the deadbolt and pulled the door open. Crossing her arms over her chest, she held the screen door open with the tip of her bare toe and held his gaze as he dismounted the bike and strode to the porch.

Stepping up onto the porch, Quinn caught Sky around the waist and lifted her off her feet, his mouth finding hers already open for his kiss. Crossing the threshold, he kicked the door closed behind them and waited as Sky turned the dead bolt. "Where?"

"Bathroom."

Quinn looked at her quizzically before walking in the direction she was pointing. He recognized the bedroom from the photos she had sent earlier and he groaned as the image of her bent over filled his mind. "You've been a very naughty girl, brat."

Sky looked up at him when he sat her on her feet. "Are you going to punish me?"

Dropping his hand to his belt, he began to unbuckle it and smiled when her cheeks flushed red. "My brother saw you. Do you think that deserves punishment?"

Sky's eyes widened and she began to back away. "Are you se...?" Seeing him hesitate, she cleared her throat and fell back into the game. "Yes, sir."

Quinn's mouth twitched as he pulled the belt free and wrapped it around his fist, leaving a few inches swinging freely. "Take off your clothes." His eyes followed the movement of her hands as she pulled her shirt up over her head and dropped it to the floor before reaching for the front closure of her bra. "Leave it. Your pants. Take them off." When her fingers fell to the button on her jeans, he bit his bottom lip and began to unbutton his own jeans, pushing them down his thighs, his eyes transfixed on the small patch of stubble covering her pussy. "Leave it like that from now on. Don't shave it anymore."

Feeling bold, Sky flattened her hand on her lower stomach and rubbed her middle finger back and forth over her clit. She watched his face as she moved her hand lower and spread herself so he could see what she was doing.

Quinn stepped forward and reached around her to turn the water on. Holding his hand beneath the shower spray, he waited for it to heat up before stepping back dropping the belt at his feet. "Get in the shower."

The teasing smile fell from Sky's face and she looked down at the belt before looking back up at him. "I thought you were going to punish me first?"

"I think you're punishing me enough for the both of us." Grasping her shoulders, he turned her and swatted her bare ass before reaching around her and unclasping her bra. Pulling her arms free of the straps, he sat the bra on the vanity before pointing at her. "Shower. Now."

Sky looked over her shoulder to ask if he would be joining her but closed her mouth and nodded when she saw him removing his own clothes. Stepping beneath the warm spray of water, she tilted her head back and closed her eyes, sighing as the water cascaded over her body. She could hear Quinn just outside the shower and her heart beat quickened when she heard him walking closer. His hand grazed her hip and she scooted to the side before running her hand over her face and through her hair. Opening her eyes, she looked up at him and waited for him to make the next move.

Quinn reached out and ran a finger over one of her breasts as he stared down into her eyes. "You are so beautiful, did ever I tell you that?"

Sky took a shaky breath and shook her head. "No."

Lightly pinching her nipple, he tugged on it until she stepped closer. "So fucking beautiful." Bending, he lowered his mouth over hers and kissed her deep, his tongue playing with hers as she fisted her hands in his hair. He lifted her up when she pressed herself against him and held her as she wrapped her legs around his waist. Her whimpers of need echoed around them and he wanted nothing more at that moment than to bury himself inside her. Breaking the kiss, he held her eyes and stared deep into her eyes. "Why did you wait so long?"

Confusion filled Sky's mind and she blinked several times before speaking. "What?"

"I've been waiting for you to decide what you wanted. I waited for you to call and you never did."

Sky unwrapped her legs and waited for him to release her before stepping back and turning to face the shower. The passion she had felt just seconds before faded away to be replaced with self doubt and fear of rejection. Picking up her loofah, she held it beneath the body wash dispenser and spoke softly, unsure if he could hear her or not. "I was scared."

Reaching around her, Quinn took the loofah from her hand. He waited as she picked up a wash cloth and soaped it up before he began washing her back while she washed between her legs. "Of what exactly?"

Looking back over her shoulder, Sky shuddered as if chilled and met Quinn's questioning gaze. "You."

Quinn's hand stopped moving and he waited for her to continue. When she didn't, he turned her around and cupped her face in his empty palm. "Why would you be scared of me, Sky? I would never do anything to maliciously hurt you. You know that, right?"

Sky nodded and turned her face into his hand, kissing his palm as she curled her fingers around his wrist. "Physically, yes. But emotionally? You have the power to hurt me, if I allow it."

"And you've decided to keep things casual, is that what you're telling me?"

Reaching up, she caught his chin with her fingertips and pulled his head down toward hers. "For now, if that's okay with you."

Quinn wanted to tell her no but clamped his teeth together when she wrapped her fingers around his semi hard cock. "Oh brat, I don't think I can argue with you while you're stroking me like that."

Raising up on her tiptoes, Sky caught his bottom lip between her teeth and nibbled as she increased her rhythm. "Good. Because right now, I want you to fuck me senseless."

Quinn released a growl and eased his hips back until she released him. "Let me clean up first and I'll fuck you until you're begging me to stop."

"That's gonna take a lot of fucking on your part, Q." Stepping around him, she slapped him on the ass before stepping from the shower and walking into her bedroom.

Quinn lifted the loofah to his nose and sniffed,

pulling a face as the scent of brown sugar and vanilla filled his senses. "Sky?"

Her voice floated in from the other room. "Yeah?"

"You uh... you have any soap that doesn't smell like a cookie?"

Poking her head back around the corner of the door, she smiled and winked at him when he turned to look at her. "Why? You scared I might gobble you up?"

His mouth dropped open and he stared at the empty doorway long after she disappeared into her room again. "Oh, brat. You are definitely getting the punishment you're asking for when I get done in here." Her titter of laughter reached his ears as he began scrubbing at his skin with the loofah, no longer caring that he'd smell like a cookie when he was done.

Sky was lying across the bed when he stepped from the bathroom. He stopped rubbing his hair with the towel he found in the linen closet and stared at the beautiful naked woman before him. She had her eyes closed and was biting down on her lower lip as her hand moved, her fingers wet with her own arousal. Dropping the towel to the floor, he lowered his hand and grasped his hard-on, stroking himself to the same rhythm as Sky's hand. A hoarse groan escaped his throat and he tightened his hand to keep from coming quickly.

Sky's hand stilled and her eyes flew open. Slamming her legs closed, she turned to her side and looked at him standing at the foot of her bed. "I didn't hear..."

"No. Don't stop." Quinn moved closer to the bed, still stroking himself, and look at her hand clamped between her thighs. "Fuck yourself for me, brat. I want to watch you make yourself come."

Sky buried her face in her pillow and shook her head. "I can't, not with you watching."

Placing a knee on the bed, Quinn reached forward and clasped one of her ankles an iron tight grip before rolling her onto her back and pulling her towards him. "Open your legs, brat?"

Sky looked down her body at him and shook her head again as she pulled her hand free of her thighs. "No."

Quinn arched an eyebrow at her and grasped her

knees. "No?" When he saw her nostrils flare, he pushed her knees apart and cupped her, sucking air through his teeth when he felt how hot she was. His finger found her wet and ready and he waited for her to tell him no again. "No?"

Closing her eyes, Sky licked her lips and arched her back as he began stroking her ever so softly. She nodded her head and her legs slammed closed, trapping his hand when she thought he'd pull away. Opening her eyes, she reached for him and ran her finger along the underside of his shaft. "I want to taste you."

Quinn gritted his teeth as she curled her fingers and grazed his balls with her nails. "If you put that mouth on me, I can almost guarantee that I'll come down your throat."

Licking her lips, Sky leaned back against her pillow and motioned him to come to her. "Then fuck me."

Quinn's smile was predatory as he wrapped his hands around her waist and pulled her to the very end of the bed. Dropping to his knees, he looked up the length of her body and held her gaze as he leaned forward and flicked his tongue against her clit. When she cried out and closed her eyes, he gently swatted her thigh and lifted his head. "Keep your eyes open, brat. Watch me while I feast on this beautiful pussy of yours." He thrust his tongue against her entrance and sighed when her essence coated his tongue. Closing his mouth over her, he hummed and cupped himself when she moaned and wiggled her hips, grinding her clit against his teeth.

"Please... please, I need to..."

Lifting his head, he licked at her, causing her to squirming and buck against his tongue. "What do you need, brat?"

In answer, Sky spread her legs wider and frantically waved her hand. "I need you. Please, Quinn. Now."

Quinn gave her a final lick before getting to his feet. "Scoot up."

Sky didn't need him to tell her twice. Using the heels of her feet, she pushed herself to the top and the bed and waited for him to join her.

"Get on your knees and face the wall." Getting fully onto the bed, Quinn walked on his knees until he was directly behind her. "Where's those handcuffs?"

Sky looked back at him, wide eyed and shook her head. "Vanilla."

Quinn couldn't hide his shock at her using her safe word. "What's wrong?"

"I don't won't feel safe being handcuffed during sex." When Quinn nodded slowly, she looked back towards the wall and waited for him to get off the bed. "I'm so..." Her breath caught in her throat as he filled her from behind. Curling her fingers around the headboard, she pressed her ass into his stomach and instantly tensed when she felt his thumb cover her asshole. She held still as he moved his thumb in a circle and rocked his hips. When his other hand wrapped in her hair she moaned began rocking her hips to the rhythm he had created.

"That's it, brat. Suck my dick with your pussy and make me come." Tightening his hold on her hair, he grabbed her thigh and increased his thrusts, driving into her harder and harder as he felt her tightening around his shaft.

Sky knew she was about to come and she didn't try to hold back. Her lower stomach began to tingle as Quinn found her g-spot and pulled at her hair, driving her closer and closer to release. Her scream of release mingled with his and her head fell forward, giving him access to the back of her neck. She shudder when he bit down on the back of her neck and thrust into her a few more times, his cum hot as it dripped down her inner thighs.

Quinn ran his hands around Sky's upper body

and cupped her breasts as he rested his head on her back. Taking deep breaths through his nose, he regulated his breathing and shook his head. "Damn it, woman."

Sky chuckled and playfully wiggled her hips. "You saying you're too tired for round two?"

Quinn growled and pinched her nipples. "Be still, wench. Give me a bit to rest up."

Sky's laughter filled the room as she maneuvered herself out from beneath him, leaving him to stretch out on the bed. "I'm going to get a quick shower and then I'll make us a pizza for supper. You like pizza, right?"

Quinn nodded and closed his eyes as he wrapped his arms around her pillow where it lay beneath his head. "I love pizza."

Sky arched an eyebrow at him and let her eyes travel down the length of his naked body. She noted the few scars that marred his perfectly tanned skin and absently wondered how he gotten them as she turned away and gathered the clothes she would wear after her shower.

Quinn's nose twitched and he opened his eyes. Confusion caused his brow to furrow as he studied the room he was in, uncertain for a minute of where he was. When he heard Sky's voice from another room, he groaned and buried his face in the pillow he was clutching. Embarrassment filled him and he silently cursed himself as he rolled over and lifted the cover Sky must have thrown over him while he slept. Quinn wasn't the type of man to sleep in a woman's bed, yet here he lay, rubbing sleep from his eyes and anticipating the pizza he remembered her mentioning. Getting to his feet, he rubbed the back of his head and made his way into the bathroom. Pulling the door closed, he looked around for his clothes and smiled when he saw them neatly folded on the vanity, a clean towel and washcloth laying next to them along with a bottle of unisex body wash.

Sky smiled when she heard the shower in her bathroom come on. Turning her head to look towards her room, she spoke into the phone. "I miss you too, Sunshine and I can't wait to see you in a few weeks."

"You sound distracted. Is... is someone there with you? Did you meet someone new and not tell me?"

Sky pressed a hand to her cheek and laughed softly. "It's not someone new. It's Quinn."

"Quinn! I thought the two if you parted ways last year? How long have you been seeing each other again?"

Sky walked into the kitchen and turned on the oven before getting the pizza from the refrigerator. "I wouldn't exactly say we're seeing each other. He..." Her woods trailed off as she tried to think of a way to tell Sunni that they were just having a little fun together.

"Damn it, my study buddy is early. Look, I've got to go but I'll call later. Love you, sis."

"I love you too." Hitting the end button, she sat

the phone on the counter and picked up the pizza pan.

"Maybe I should leave?"

Sky's entire body jumped and the pizza threatened to spill to the floor. Clutching a hand to her chest, she turned and faced Quinn. "You scared the crap out of me sneaking up like that."

Quinn continued rolling his shirt sleeves up and nodded his head in the direction of her phone. "Didn't want to interrupt the phone call with your boyfriend. Wouldn't want to cause trouble for you."

Sky looked up from putting the pizza in the oven and slowly straightened to her full height as she closed the oven door. "Boyfriend? Why would you think I had a boyfriend?" When Quinn dipped his head in the direction of her phone again, Sky crossed her arms and leaned a jean clad hip against the counter. "You were eavesdropping?"

Shaking his head no, Quinn ran his hands down the front of his freshly laundered shirt. "Just the end. By the way, thanks for washing my clothes. You didn't have to do that."

Sky shrugged and pointed to her phone. "Care to see who I was talking to?"

Quinn again shook his head. "It's really none of my business."

"Oh, but it is. Quinn, I don't want you thinking I'm the sort of woman that cheats."

Quinn rubbed the bridge of his nose and sighed heavily. "I never said that."

"But you insinuated it. You could've just asked who I had been talking to and I would've told you the truth. I was talking to my sister." When Quinn's head shot up, Sky's heart skipped a beat. "If I didn't know any better, Q, I'd think you cared for me." Lifting her hand up, she squinted and held her forefinger and thumb apart. "Just a smidge."

Quinn's arm shot out and he clutched her wrist and pulled her against his hard body. "You're being a cheeky wench again, brat."

"I actually think this time... you're the one being the brat." Sky laughed out loud and pushed herself free of his embrace when his chest rumbled against hers. "Feisty. I like it."

Quinn shook his head at her as his mouth lifted in a lopsided smile. "You're going to be handful, aren't you?"

Winking at him, she turned and pulled open the refrigerator door. "I always am, sir."

Chapter 19

"I think I want it over there against that wall."

Quinn turned his head slowly and glared at Sky. "We already tried it over there and you didn't like it." Dropping his end of the dresser, he motioned for Declan to lower his end to the floor. "This is where it's going and if you don't like it, you can move the son of a bitch yourself."

Declan looked from his brother to Sky and back again. "I'm just going to go see if there's something to drink in the house. I'll..." He stopped speaking when he realized neither of them were paying him any attention. "All right then."

Sky had her hands propped on her hips and she was glaring daggers at Quinn. "I don't want it there, bossy. I want the damn thing over against the other wall."

"And I'm telling you right now, I'm not moving it again." Quinn swallowed back a laugh when he noticed her face turning red as she began tapping her foot. "You are getting a might big for your britches little lady."

Sky's mouth dropped open and she dropped her arms to her side as she balled her hands into tight fists. "*Are you calling me fat?*"

"No, but that mouth is going to get that ass spanked if you keep it up." When he noticed her mouth twitch, his eyes widened as understanding settled in. "You brazen hussy! You're trying to get spanked."

Smirking, Sky reached up and pulled the necklace up and let the pendent fall against her chest. "Took you long enough to figure it out, *Quinn*."

Stuffing his hands in his back pocket, Quinn narrowed his eyes at her before nodding. "That's strike one, brat."

Turning, Sky closed the bedroom door and turned the lock before reaching up and unbuttoning the strap of her overall's as she walked towards the bed. The baggy overall's fell around her ankles when she unbuttoned the second strap and she leaned over the foot of the bed, her bare ass arched high as she looked back at the man on the opposite side of the room. "Quinn."

"Strike two." His hand lowered to his belt and he pulled it through his belt loops after unbuckling it. When her lips formed his name again, he smiled at her and started across the room, wrapping the belt around his fist and biting his bottom lip in anticipation of things to come.

Thank you for purchasing Petals & Steel.

I am extremely grateful to everyone that made the decision to purchase and read one of my books.

I hope that it was everything you hoped it would be. It would be really nice if you could share this book with your friends and family by posting to **Facebook, Instagram** or by creating a **TikTok** video.

If you enjoyed Petals & Steel, I'd like to hear from you and hope that you could take some time to post a review on **Amazon** and/or **Goodreads.**

About the Author

Greer Rylie is from small town Arkansas and has been happily married for 24 years, showing her commitment to her Southern values. She loves cooking and makes delicious Southern dishes in her kitchen. She also enjoys taking photos, capturing beautiful moments. Greer cares deeply about animals, which reflects her kind personality. She's written four books, and has several more planned to be released at a later date. She dreams of becoming a best-selling author and sharing her stories with more people. Join Greer on her journey as she continues to write the stories she hopes you'll fall in love with.

facebook.com/GreerRylie.Author

tiktok.com/@greer.rylieauthor21

amazon.com/Greer-Rylie/e/B09NCKP6C3

instagram.com/greer_rylie_writes